DREAMING OF HIS PEN PAL'S KISS

Cowboy Mountain Christmas

Book 6

JESSIE GUSSMAN

Contents

Acknowledgments

Cover art by Lara Wynter
Editing by Heather Hayden
Narration by Jay Dyess
Author Services by CE Author Assistant

Listen to the unabridged audio for FREE performed by Jay Dyess on the Say with Jay channel on YouTube. Get early access to all of Jay's recordings and listen to Jessie's books before they're available to the general public, plus get daily Bible readings by Jay and bonus scenes by becoming a Say with Jay channel member.

Chapter One

"Is that another name for your pen pal program?" Journee asked her dad while seated across the desk from him in his church office in Mistletoe, Arkansas.

"It is."

Her dad, glasses perched on the end of his nose, his salt-and-pepper hair not nearly as thick as it used to be, tapped the desk in front of him with one finger, as though thinking.

Journee's stomach shivered, just a little, for some odd reason. She already had four people she was writing to in the church's new pen pal program. But out of those four people, only one had written her more than once.

She wondered if she came on too strong in her original letter. Maybe she just didn't write the kind of letters people wanted to respond to. Maybe people were too busy. She didn't want to admit to her failure, but she had to admit to being discouraged.

Her dad, Pastor Race, tilted his head and narrowed his eyes just a little, as though he were thinking. Or as though he knew what she was going to say before she said it. Which was most likely the case.

Her mouth opened anyway, and the words he probably knew were going to come out spilled. "I can take the name."

"I haven't even told you whether it's a man or woman." Humor laced his words, along with a heavy dose of affection.

She'd lost her parents when she was pretty young, and it was funny how she had nothing but good memories of them. Like her brain had completely blanked out and recorded over anything bad that had ever happened.

Still, Race and Penny had adopted her and her five siblings, and she honestly had nothing but good memories of them either. It wasn't that everything that had ever happened in her life had been good, other than her parents being killed a car accident, but God had blessed her with two sets of wonderful parents.

She wasn't quite sure why, when some people didn't even get one.

"Dad, you know it doesn't matter. I just love writing people. Or maybe, I just love writing in general. And things really get slow in the ER at night. I have plenty of time."

The ER in a small town was an odd thing. For days, they'd go with barely a soul showing up, and then one night, they might have nothing but chaos all night long.

Most of the time though, it was quiet and she had plenty of time to daydream or, as she'd been doing, write her letters.

"I know you do. I just don't want to give you more than you can handle." He tapped his finger some more. "Although, while I do have at least forty people writing from the church, I have more requests for partners than I do people to match them with. I was almost thinking of writing to this person myself."

Whoever it was, they would definitely benefit from writing to her dad more than they would from writing to her. She'd never met a wiser person.

"Maybe that's what the Lord would want you to do."

Race shook his head slightly. "Actually, when the name first came in, I thought of you immediately. I probably would have asked you to do it then if I didn't know you were already paired up with four people."

"Dad, I can do it. Especially if you think I should. If you think it's meant for me." She tried to keep the hope out of her voice. All of her siblings except Shawn, who would probably never get married, had found God's plan for them and, at the same time, found a lifetime love.

It was her fondest hope.

She thought she'd had it with her high school sweetheart.

Thoughts of Alex turned the excited shiver in her stomach into something which felt more like congealed gravy.

Thoughts of Alex didn't hurt anymore, but they made her sad.

Because she viewed him as a big mistake.

And wished she wouldn't have wasted so much time on him when she was younger. Maybe she'd missed God's plan and God's big love story for her because she'd been focused on the wrong guy— because she'd definitely been focused on Alex.

Or maybe Alex had been right for her, and he just hadn't been strong enough to stand up to his parents and say so.

But she didn't want a man who wasn't respectful to his parents, and she admired him in an odd kind of way for listening to them.

Still, it was hard not to think of what might have been.

Her dad didn't answer for a moment, and she gave him time. He'd warned her from the beginning that Alex probably wasn't right for her. Not in so many words, but anytime she'd gone to him for advice, his advice would have turned her away from Alex.

To her shame, she hadn't usually listened and hadn't gone to him as much as she probably should have anyway.

Her dad breathed deeply and straightened the pen in front of him that was already straight before looking up at her. "This was a little different. And I think there's potential on both ends for things to go badly, so while I know that you have never had a problem obeying the rules, I'm going to remind you. It is imperative that you not use your real name and that you not ask for theirs."

She nodded. She'd not broken any of the pen pal program's rules, and she didn't plan to.

"It's also important that you don't give too many identifying details about your life."

He smiled, the love he felt for her reaching deep inside and swirling around her chest. From the very beginning, she'd never had a doubt about how Race and Penny felt about her. It was amazing that they loved her no matter how stupid she was. How many dumb mistakes she made. And how often she messed up and didn't listen.

After the debacle with Alex, she couldn't imagine her dad giving her advice that she didn't follow.

"I suppose I'm a little overprotective of you, because not only are you my daughter, but you're the youngest. I know you're all grown up now, able to support yourself, and you don't need your old dad anymore..."

"I need you, Dad. Don't ever say that I don't. I would have avoided a lot of heartache in my life if I would have listened to you."

"Water under the bridge." He shook his head and reached his hand out across the desk. She put hers in it easily. Race and Penny had never hesitated to hug them or touch them, and she appreciated it. It was part of what made her feel loved.

"Regardless. Your advice means everything to me. Whatever you say, I'll do it to the best of my ability."

"Thank you. I know you will. You were such an easy child to raise. And you've grown into such a wonderful woman. But I don't want to see you hurt. And..." He looked down at the name in front of him. "I think this person is vulnerable too. I know you would never do anything to harm them on purpose, and I don't think that most people would look at this person and see how fragile they are, but I just want you both to be careful. At least for a year. If you're still writing after that time, I think it would be safe to say you could probably open up a little more."

He said the last slowly, like he hadn't quite thought it through. His eyes were on the calendar, and Journee's eyes landed there too.

February seventh.

The rest of the world would be celebrating Valentine's Day tomorrow, but not in Mistletoe, Arkansas. For them, it was Christmas year-round.

"I don't have a problem with that, Dad. No identifying details, and no names, and no real address, until we've been writing for a year."

She looked down, running her finger over the picture frame on her dad's desk that held the first picture of their family that had ever been taken. Race and Penny stood behind them with Ethan, whom they'd never adopted but had lived with them for a while, with Journee and her five siblings in front.

A hodgepodge of people maybe, but she loved that picture, because it represented a new beginning. She thought her birth parents would smile at where their children had landed and what God had done for them.

Still, Race hesitated, and she felt she needed to say something. "Dad, if you don't think that this is something I should do, don't give it to me."

He was silent for a bit, although the air around them was alive. Sounds of children from the daycare playing on the playground outside came muffled through the window, and ladies' laughter from the Bible study down the hall seemed to seep under the door.

That was one of her favorite things about the church. She could go into the sanctuary and just feel the stillness and peace of God, and she could walk out of the sanctuary and feel the life and breath of the saints who made up the church.

It was just a building, but it always felt alive to her. Always gave her peace. Comfort. And hope.

Finally, Race shifted and swallowed. "No. I actually know this is something you should do." Concern overshadowed every other emotion on his face. "I want to protect you. I know your heart was already broken, and love can be hard sometimes. Not that I'm expecting you to fall in love with this person."

He tapped the paper on the desk. "Not romantic love. But even friends can break your heart. I just can't help but think that even though I know this is what you're supposed to do, there's going to be tears ahead. As a father, I don't want that. Still, I know that sometimes it's the hard times in our life where we grow the most. It's what God uses to bring us closer to Him and to make us into the people that he wants us to be. I can definitely look back over my own life and see that as a stark reality. The hardest times of my life ended up being the best times for me. It's just...they're so hard to walk through. But I think even more than that, it's hard to watch people we love walk through them. If you love someone, their pain is yours. So, if I'm hesitating, maybe it's about my own heart as much as it's about yours."

Journee smiled at that. Her dad wasn't more concerned about himself than her, but he was also a humble man, and he wouldn't boast. "I love that you care about me. And I know I am a dreamer. I know I have a tendency to make really bad decisions, but I think I'm doing better, and I'm also stronger than what I get credit for. I might be the youngest, but I am grown up."

She didn't really mind the tendency of everyone in her family to treat her like she was still a child. In some ways, she kinda felt like she was.

She had made some foolish choices. Although, at least for the way some people thought, she'd made a wise decision in completing her four-year nursing degree, but she'd passed up a lot more lucrative opportunities in order to come back to her hometown and settle down. She had no desire to leave her family and friends in the town she grew up in.

None.

"I know you do."

At that, Race pushed back away from the desk and came around. Journee stood, and he embraced her, the strength of his arms and the scent of his aftershave familiar and beloved, comforting, making her feel safe like she always did when Race hugged her. She knew he'd protect her with everything he had, but she also knew she was an adult and had to be responsible for her own decisions and her own life.

He squeezed her for a bit and pulled away first. "Here's the address. It's a man. He's not retired. And, like all of the other pen pal recipients in our program, he's in the hospital. He hasn't been in quite as long as most of the others, only a couple of weeks, but because of the nature of his job, people who care about him know that being in the hospital is psychologically excruciating for him. They felt that giving him a pen pal—someone like you," Race said with a smile, "is what he needs to get himself back to where he needs to be in order to do his job to the best of his ability."

"Are you saying he's depressed?" She tilted her head, having had some experience with depression in her schooling. Also, Alex had been going to be a psychologist.

"I don't think he's there. Yet. I do think it's a distinct possibility, especially if he doesn't get better." Race's words were slightly hesitant, like he didn't want to say too much.

Journee nodded. She didn't need to know all the details. She had a good imagination, and she could fill them in with whatever she wanted. She could have a conversation with herself. Or with a reluctant man who needed to be encouraged. Of course, she had been worried she came on too strong with her other pen pals. Maybe she should start slowly.

"I'll do my best, Dad."

"I knew you would, Journee. I love you." He squeezed her again before letting go.

She fingered the paper as she walked out of his office. Somehow, the idea of this pen pal, and writing to this man, stirred threads of excitement that she hadn't had when her dad had handed her the addresses to the other people.

She had a feeling...this man was going to be different.

Chapter Two

The dream began the way it always did.

He was on the field, and he'd just caught the ball, both hands wrapped around it, tucking it in the crook of his arm, securing it, in the split second before he made the ninety-degree turn and headed straight up the field.

He always caught the ball in the dream.

He never fumbled it, either.

Considering how the rest of the dream worked out, it was always slightly amazing that the beginning of the dream was so positive.

But he got to the inevitable part where his legs wouldn't work.

There was no pain. No blood. No ripping metal, shattering glass, screaming. Nothing. Even the stands were silent.

In the dream.

But his legs just wouldn't move. He couldn't get them to go. He could see the defense converging. See the helmet lowered for the hit that would end his career. Feel that sharp twist of nerves in his stomach, the one that overrode the aggression and determination and grit that had gotten him through junior high and high school and college ball. Although he hadn't been drafted, he'd been signed as a free agent and had clawed his way to a starting position, the first time in his life he'd been paid to play football.

Then, through hard work and determination, he'd become the best at his position. The best tight end in the league.

His hands were sure. He never dropped the ball, and he wasn't afraid to lay out, to create big blocks for the running back behind him. Every single skill that was necessary for him to excel in his position was a skill he mastered.

But in the dream, his legs wouldn't work.

He stood frozen, helpless as the defenders reached him. A linebacker first. A big hit, but he'd stay on his feet. His legs wouldn't move, but the defenders couldn't get him down.

Not at first.

A smaller cornerback hit him next, fast and tough, but he still didn't fall. Didn't touch the dirt. The play wasn't dead.

Not until the second and third linebacker slammed into him, and in the dream, he didn't feel the pain, the hits didn't hurt.

Until they did.

And somehow, he was on the ground, bleeding, and the worst part, his leg, the thigh bone bent at an odd angle, blood soaking his uniform, the horrified eyes looking out through the other team's helmets.

And then the horrified eyes of his buddies on his own team. His friends. His homies. The guys he did everything with. In season and out of season. Man, he even vacationed with some of them.

But now, in the dream, he lay on the ground, his leg twisted, and the pain began, shooting up and down his leg, out his arms, through his fingertips, pounding in his head, but the worst pain was his heart.

Because when he looked at his buddies and held his hand out, asking for a hand up, they looked at him in horror, shaking their heads and turning away.

Suddenly, the stadium was empty, and he was there alone, bleeding and unable to move, unable to get up...

And there was no one to help.

That's when he woke up. That's when he *always* woke up.

Even after a little nap in the middle of the day, sunlight streaming in through the hospital window, beeping coming down the hall, his door half cracked... The lights were out, but the hospital never slept.

Therefore, neither did he. Not even at night. People bustling in all day long—he was a hot commodity after all, and no one wanted to see anything happen to him.

They didn't know that the dream, or nightmare as it was, had become his biggest fear.

Being alone.

He stirred, shaking the last remnants of the dream from his head, and the paper that lay on his chest, the one he'd been reading when he dozed off, crinkled.

He gripped it, not in a normal way, and he made his fingers relax.

Funny, he was in the hospital because of a car accident, but that was never a part of his dream.

The injury, and the traction devices on his leg right now, were not from a football injury but from the car accident.

His dream always had it messed up.

Running a hand down over his eyes and across his cheeks where the stubble scratched his palm, he took a breath and tried to gather himself.

He wasn't alone. He would never be alone. It was something he'd been taught in Sunday School, although it had been a while since he'd been in church.

Still, he supposed it was a natural feeling of people who didn't have stable families.

He'd seen it in his teammates, seen it in the way they self-medicated.

Some of them had enough natural talent that it didn't matter.

He'd never been able to do that. He knew, if he took his focus off football, even for a second, someone else would have his job.

He hadn't gotten to where he was because of talent.

He'd gotten there because of determination, and sacrifice, and hard work, and the grit to never quit, to do what no one else would do, to work when everyone else stopped, to push himself where no one else would go, because without football, his life was a mess.

Dante Tolzien held the paper in his hand open in front of his face, adjusting his body, ignoring the throbbing, sharp pain that burned up his leg.

Sometimes, if he was very still, he could get the pain to stop. He'd heard there were switches in his brain where he could turn the pain on and off.

Most of his success had been mental, so he believed it.

It was something he'd been working on in the long hours as he lay in the hospital bed, with nothing to do but watch TV and occasionally talk to the guys who came to see him, although most of them had gone home after they'd lost their last playoff game in January, and the coaches as well, the ones who weren't fired or who hadn't left, but he'd not been kept up to date because the season was over.

There'd be the normal shakeups, position changes, trades, new draft picks, and retirements.

But he had every intention of continuing to play for the Galveston Grizzlies through the rest of his contract and had no reason to think that the team would cut him, unless he couldn't keep up in training camp.

He had a few months.

His eyes focused on the handwriting on the paper—whimsical curls and loops screaming the author was a woman, long before he'd gotten to her signature.

One of his coaches had signed him up for some kind of pen pal program. He hadn't known. He certainly wasn't interested in replying.

The woman obviously had no idea he was a football player, and he would guess, from the tone of her letter, that she knew nothing about football and even less about sports in general.

He wasn't interested. He wanted a woman who understood him.

"Hey there, Dante," Coach Jacobs said as he walked in the room.

Tim Jacobs wasn't actually a coach. He was more of a coach's assistant. Coach Shea, who coached the offensive line, was the coach that Coach Jacobs most often worked under.

There were a lot of personnel involved in making a professional team successful.

Dante loved the family-like atmosphere. But he wasn't fooled. It was all about money, and as soon as the money didn't flow, people left. Or got fired.

Coach Jacobs had been around as long as he had been—six years. Which was an eternity in professional football.

"Hey, Coach."

"Could have used you today. Got some guys that think because they've got 'professional ballplayer' beside their name they don't have to work anymore. Needed an old-timer who can show them that's not true."

Dante grinned, reaching up and bumping Coach Jacob's fist as he stopped by the side of the bed. "I'm an old-timer?" He said it with humor in his voice, but he cringed inside. Twenty-eight was old for a professional ballplayer. Most guys didn't last past five years. And here he was having completed six.

His body felt every second of those six years. Plus the four years of college before that. And on and on.

"Yeah, got a bunch of kids here looking at the team and thinking they can make it big-time based on talent alone. You try to tell them different, but most of 'em don't pay attention."

Dante nodded. He'd seen it. Same as everyone else. Technically, the season was over, most of the guys scattered.

Dante didn't have family, so he hung out in Galveston during the off-season. He and Coach Jacobs were as good friends as a coach and a player could be, he supposed. Eventually, he'd like to coach too.

He'd probably end up starting at an assistant position the way Coach Jacobs had. His professional career hadn't been as star-studded as Dante's though, so maybe he'd be offered a better position straight out of the gate.

He definitely didn't want to be an announcer, the way so many ballplayers ended up.

He didn't want to be in front of a camera, speaking. He wanted to get his hands dirty in the action. If he couldn't play, coaching was the next best thing.

"See you got a letter. The Big Dude signed you up for that."

Coach Samuels. The head coach. Everybody called him The Big Dude.

"Coach Samuels? Why?"

Coach Samuels did some odd things, mostly based on his religion, similar to Tony Dungy maybe, although Coach Dungy was before Dante's time. Still, he'd heard the comparisons and figured them to be accurate.

"He thought you needed it. He and the guy who runs that program went to college together back in the day. Stone ages, I guess, for you. Coach was worried about you, still is. Up here." Coach Jacobs tapped his head.

Dante pressed his lips together and looked away. There was nothing wrong with his head.

"It's my leg that's broken. He's worried about the wrong end." He forced a smile and tried to put a little glint in his eye. One he definitely didn't feel any more than surface deep.

"Can't disagree with you. You've got the best attitude of anyone I've ever seen lying in this stinkin' place for so long."

"It's only been a couple of weeks."

"Long enough. Anyway, you know when The Big Dude gets an idea in his head, it's best to just go with it. He wants you to answer that. Thinks it'll be good for you."

Dante shifted and tried not to grimace at the pain that seized his leg and ran up his side. "Does he realize it's a woman?"

"Pretty sure he does. And a woman who isn't involved in sports. At all. I'm pretty sure when The Big Dude talked to the fella in charge of that, those were his specific requests."

"Those are exactly the things I don't want."

It was like Coach was doing it just to be a jerk.

Although Dante knew better.

Coach Samuels was just as much of a father to him as anyone had ever been. More maybe. Not that he wouldn't hesitate to trade him or cut him if that turned out to be best for the team, but he was the kind of coach that Dante could stay in touch with for the rest of his life and would know the man would care about him. He was just that kind of guy.

Coach Jacobs stayed for a little longer while they chatted and discussed plays and personnel moves and things that would affect their year next year and their chances of making it to the championship game.

By the time Coach Jacobs left, Dante was tired but not sleepy, and the paper in his hand was soft and crinkled from his hand gripping it.

The Big Dude wouldn't ask him to do anything that wasn't in his very best interest. Not to mention, even in the off-season, one didn't say no to the head coach.

He lifted his hand, and even though he'd already read the letter twice, he read it once more.

Dear Pen Pal,

I suppose some people would sit and stare at a blank page and wonder what in the world they'd say to a stranger.

It probably tells you everything that you ever need to know about me that I had to sort through all of the things I wanted to say and pick out the things I thought would be the most important.

I could fill this page up, and a whole notebook too, just chatting.

Somehow, I think that would bore you more than it would inspire you, so I tried to think of something that I could say to a man who is in the hospital that would be even a little bit interesting. It was a little hard since I know nothing else about you.

Of course, the top thing that comes to mind is that I'm a nurse.

I'm laughing right now, because that either made you happy, or it made you decide not to write me back.

People don't seem to have neutral opinions about nurses.

Funny, because it's all about our experience and not really about individual nurses. In other words, we don't hate a nurse because she's not nice, we hate a nurse because we had a nurse who wasn't nice. Make sense?

Or we hate nurses because we hate being in the hospital. That's possible too.

If it makes you feel any better, I'm also currently in the hospital right now.

Unfortunately, I'm in the hospital because I choose to be, while I understand you don't have a choice.

Regardless, you are the fifth person that I am attempting to become pen pals with.

All four of my other pen pals puttered out to the point where I don't think they're writing me anymore.

I think it might have something to do with me being

overwhelming and those myriads of notebooks that I could fill up just chatting about nothing and being completely entertained.

I'm starting to realize, though, it doesn't entertain anyone else.

The one other thing that I can tell you is that I live in Arkansas. I can't give you my town, and the address you write back to is a PO box in a different town. That mail is forwarded to me.

I know it's almost Valentine's Day, but I love Christmas, and the town I live in is a great place to live if you love Christmas.

What do you love?

Sincerely,

The Healing Pen

Chapter Three

Hey, Healing Pen,

Thank you for not writing a notebook full of random stuff. You're right. I wouldn't have read it.

You're also right about nurses. I guess I belong in the second category, which was bad experiences.

Not that any of my nurses are not kind, they just... aren't always professional, if you know what I mean.

I'll admit right up front that I'm only writing because someone I trust signed me up, and I feel like I have to.

I have two loves. The one I'm not gonna talk about. The other is computers.

Best regards,
Computer Nerd

❄

*J*ournee held the slip of paper in her hand. He hadn't needed to waste a whole piece of paper on the few lines he'd written.

She felt like this was going to end up being a dead end. Obviously, the guy wasn't the slightest bit interested in writing to her.

At least his handwriting was neat, each letter perfectly formed. Not the kind of handwriting she would have guessed for a man.

She looked around the quiet house that she shared with her parents and siblings, Shawn and Blakely. The two children, Darcy and Frank, that Penny and Race were currently fostering lived with them as well. However, there'd been a Valentine's Day party at Mistletoe's community center, and Penny and Race had taken Darcy and Frank there.

She supposed she never thought she'd make it to twenty-eight and be spending Valentine's Day alone.

She also thought it was probably a girl thing. But of all the days of the year where she thought about what could have been, Valentine's Day was the day.

Knowing if she didn't distract herself she'd soon be depressed and looking for chocolate, she set the letter down and reached for her pen. Obviously, the man didn't want to write to her but was being forced to. Still, she wasn't going to let what he did dictate what she did.

If he wanted to answer her with one-word sentences, that was up to him. But as long as he wrote to her, she'd write back, and she'd do her best to be who she was. Because she never really saw any reason to be anything different.

Dear Computer Nerd,

I guess that I could go on a personal crusade to change your mind about nurses, but it sounds like maybe that's what caused the problem to begin with. Or something like that.

I'm a little confused when you say you love computers. Is it that you love the way they look? Or you love to use computers? Or you love working on computers? That was really open for interpretation, and since it's the one thing you told me, I'd really like to be clear about it. If it's not too much trouble.

I actually don't own a computer. I know that's weird, because everybody has one, although I do have a smartphone. I don't really like it, though.

I like doing what I'm doing right now, which is putting pen on paper, just saying what I think.

Next week is Valentine's Day, and everyone around me says I'm a bit of a romantic. Actually, that's not true.

Everyone around me says I am a terrible romantic, a hopeless romantic.

I suppose they're right. It's funny how people looking outside of us can sometimes see us better than we can see ourselves, but they can never know exactly what's going on in our head. I think we think so much there's just no way that we could even tell everyone all of our thoughts.

It'd be overwhelming, as you pointed out. No one would ever pay attention.

So, I'm assuming you are probably spending Valentine's Day in the hospital, which is sad. I'm also going to assume that you're not a hopeless romantic and probably you're whatever the opposite is of a hopeless romantic.

I was trying to think of a middle ground for us. You love computers, and I don't own one, so that's out.

I'm a nurse, and you hate them, so that's out.

How do you feel about sheep?

Sincerely,

The Healing Pen

Hi Healing Pen,

You're right. I spent Valentine's Day in the hospital.

Probably because of that, my opinion of nurses has not changed.

I'm sorry, I guess I was in kind of a bad mood, and I resented the fact that I had to write to someone I didn't even know, simply because someone else wanted me to. When I said I love computers, I meant I'm working on building an app.

It's actually something I do in my spare time. I'm into coding and have written a couple, but nothing that's taken off. Not that it has to take off in order for me to consider it worthwhile. It's just once I had mine ready, someone else had already done it and had been more successful than me.

I'll have to get back to you on the sheep question. I've never thought about them.

Best regards,

Computer Nerd

Dear Computer Nerd,

You've never thought about sheep? Don't you count them at night when you can't sleep? I guess that's what I was thinking. Other than the fact that lambs are cute. But lambs, like every other baby animal, grow up, so I wouldn't actually want one. But if I had to count sheep, I suppose I would picture a lamb in my mind, because it's more fun to count cute things, right?

I'm sorry Valentine's Day did not improve your opinion of nurses. I think I'm starting to understand what the problem is, which, I have to admit, makes me more curious about you.

I think there are a lot of things you're not telling me.

I think I like that because I think I'd rather not know.

The idea of an app is super cool. What kind of app?
Sincerely,
The Healing Pen

Hey Healing Pen,
I guess that was my negative attitude coming out again, although Valentine's Day really did stink here.

I don't even like chocolate.

The app I was working on tracks stats. Sports stats, team stats, and individual player stats, but I wanted it to be all-encompassing—basically, any stat you ever wanted would be on the app.

It was a pretty big thing, but someone else has already done it.

I'm still working on it, just because I like it, but it will probably never get published, because, like I said, it's already been done.

I guess I'm back to the drawing board. It's okay. I have plenty of time to think here. It's going to be another week before I could even consider going home. Not that I'm in a big rush to go there. I still won't be allowed to go anywhere.

No offense, but I'm looking forward to getting out and being able to do more than watch TV and write letters.

I suppose it's been kind of rude of me not to ask you what you like to do. Other than write letters and be a nurse.

Best regards,
Computer Geek

Chapter Four

Journee stared at the paper in front of her. Normally when she got a letter, she wrote back within three or four days. Computer Geek had been doing the same, whether because he wanted to or because he was being made to, she wasn't sure. But that way, both of them got a letter a week.

Still, she could hardly name the emotion that vacillated in her chest. She refused to label it hurt. She didn't even like the guy, not much anyway, so he couldn't hurt her.

Disappointment? Maybe that was it. She had high hopes for having a fun pen pal relationship. Nothing romantic, just a fun friendship through letters.

But the guy seemed closed off and distant.

In this last letter...she looked down at it on her desk, where it had sat for the last ten days.

It was like he was forcing himself to ask something about her. Really? He was so uninterested in writing and in her and in having anything to do with her that he had to be like, *oh yeah, I guess I'm being rude not to ask anything about you. Not that I want to know.*

She shouldn't take it personally. It wasn't her job to be his best friend. It was her job to cheer him up. And she hadn't been doing that well.

Obviously, the man wasn't interested in anything she was interested in. So, she supposed it was up to her to be interested in what he was.

But what was that? The other thing he loved he couldn't tell her, and she couldn't get upset with it because the terms of the pen pal relationship were to not disclose any details of their personal life. Even her saying she was a nurse might have gone a little close to that line, although there were lots of nurses in the country. It wasn't exactly an identifying characteristic.

She racked her brain as she had been doing for ten days to find something, anything, that she could talk to the man about that wouldn't allow the irritation that she felt at his less-than-complimentary question to show through.

Maybe he was shy. She hadn't considered that. Maybe he didn't know how to ask without feeling like he was being rude or pushy.

Maybe he just wasn't a very good writer and didn't know how to phrase things so that it didn't hurt her feelings.

Always think the best of people. Assume the best in their motivations.

Race had told all of them that throughout their teen years. He was right as always. It did make things go more smoothly, when one assumed the best about others.

She would go with it, because it was right. She needed to assume the best and not be offended over stupid things.

But what to say?

It was two days later before she finally figured something out. She actually thought it was a really great idea.

But she supposed she'd have to wait and see what Computer Geek thought.

Hopefully, he wrote back quickly.

Dear Computer Geek,

I have an idea for an app.

As far as I know, and I looked it up online, no one else is doing anything like this.

Ready?

What if you made a hospital app?

I know you don't like nurses, but what if there was an app to rate nurses? Or at least to rate hospitals and rate the service that you feel you're getting in the hospital?

I think you'd have to be careful, because you wouldn't want to make anyone mad or hurt anyone's feelings, but it could be kind of like stats for sports figures? You could include doctors in it too.

Even the food…you could have a place to rate the quality of the TV or the physical therapists. Really, the sky is the limit.

And as a nurse, I think it would inspire me to want to do better. Of course, I wouldn't like reviews or comments that weren't complimentary, but it could be like restaurant reviews. Everybody has their own opinion.

Anyway, I thought of it and thought you might be interested.

It's just a thought, but it might give people in hospitals something to do.

You never did get back to me on the sheep question.

I'm not sure you get winter where you are, but if you do, I'm hoping you enjoy spring. It's beautiful here in the Ozark foothills.

Sincerely,

The Healing Pen

Dear Healing Pen,

I loved your idea!

That's why it's taken me so long to write back. I actually started the day I got your letter—I'd gone home the day before and was already bored out of my mind—on working on the app that you suggested.

It was a brilliant idea. And you're right, there's nothing like it.

And why not? Shouldn't doctors and nurses be held to the same standard that everyone else is? You can rate restaurants, hotels, B&Bs, books, movies...why not healthcare?

So anyway, it's been two weeks, and I actually have a bit of a prototype that I thought you'd be interested in trying.

Now, I know you don't have a computer, and I know we're not supposed to send detailed information. The man who set us up on my end told me that much. However, if you send me your email address, I'll give you a link where you can try out my app. I'm still developing it, but you can give me some feedback.

I think I'm a no on the sheep. I don't want to be a sheep. I want to make my own way. I think people sometimes just hear stuff and believe it, and they're afraid to branch out from their little bubble and listen to anything that doesn't agree with what they already believe or to be different from everyone around them.

I don't want that ever to be me.

I've never really fit in anywhere, so the sheep thing isn't for me.

You never answered my question. What do you like to do other than write letters and be a nurse?

Thanks.

Computer Geek

Dear Computer Geek,

Wow! You already know I don't know anything about computers, but I am so impressed with what you've done. I cannot believe you made this app yourself.

I can see how it's handy and informative. I can also see how people could use it just for enjoyment. I mean, you could actually build like the ideal hospital, right! You know, picking the best doctors and nurses from each hospital in the country once the app has been filled in.

One suggestion, I know you said this is just a skeleton, but I do hope you have room for comments. Because, say for example you rate a nurse a three, and you do that because you don't like her suggestive bedside manner.

That same nurse might get a five from me, because I wouldn't have that problem. So, to explain why you put the rating down you did would be very helpful.

I'm really excited about this! I think you've got something really cool on your hands.

Obviously, when I'm not in the ER, and even when I am—I'm in it now, but it's a quiet night—I enjoy writing. Not stories, because they're too long. I don't have the patience to build a world, but I just like writing my thoughts down. I suppose some people talk, and that's fine, but I never did, not much. As the youngest of six siblings, I had to be pretty loud if I wanted to be heard.

So I just sat in a corner and wrote.

I live in the Ozarks. We have all kinds of rivers and streams, waterfalls, and just beautiful glens with rippling brooks, and I'm fascinated with water. I suppose, if I weren't a nurse, I would be a whitewater rafting guide.

You?

Sincerely,

The Healing Pen

Dear Healing Pen,

I had been going in a totally different direction with the app. Much more serious. But I like the way you think. Actually, I think there could be a game associated with it, completely separate from the app but connected, if that makes sense. I know it wouldn't be for everyone, but for people who are stuck in hospitals, it could have appeal for them.

Not to mention someone in a hospital in Phoenix could connect with someone in a hospital in Maine. I think it's nice when you find people whom you have things in common with. Isn't that what we look for in people? Similarities.

I guess, don't tell anyone, but this is where I probably owe you an apology.

When you first wrote to me, all I saw were our differences.

I wasn't very nice. I guess I could say I was in pain, still am actually. It's a pretty painful thing to break your femur. But I don't think I can blame my unkindness on it.

Or maybe I should say I don't want to.

I don't want to be the kind of person who can't be friends with someone who is different than they are.

I know you didn't say anything, and I could be wrong, but I don't think you probably would ever say anything.

But I was rude.

And I'm sorry.

You came up with a really great idea, and you shared it. I assume you were looking for something that you and I could talk about that I wouldn't be mean to you about.

Anyway, just this experience with the app showed me maybe that you're a better person than I am but also that I want to be a better person.

Thanks for that.

Thanks for doing it without hitting me over the head with a sermon or a bunch of Bible verses. You wouldn't have gotten very far if you did that.

Okay, I just needed to get that off my chest. I felt it was right to tell you. You've done a lot for me, with just the idea of the app, and then your feedback. Maybe it'll never go anywhere. Regardless, if it does, I have you to thank.

I'm going to spend some time working on it and adding to it, and I'll email you another link.

I had thought, when you sent me your email address, that we would write that way. It would be easier. But sometimes I think easier isn't always better. Actually, I kind of like going to my mailbox now and wondering if there will be a letter from you in there.

Not sure why this person in my life wanted me to start writing to you, but it's funny how little things can give us something to look forward to and lift our mood. Maybe that's what he intended.

If it is, it worked.

Thanks for hanging in there with me.

I think whitewater rafting sounds like fun.

Gratefully,

Computer Geek

Dear Computer Geek,

The best time to go whitewater rafting is in the spring, when the rivers are high.

I'm just telling you what I found out, because I've never actually been whitewater rafting. Before you say anything, I know I said that I would be a whitewater rafting guide.

But that was just whimsical thinking. Because obviously, my life didn't go that way, and it will not happen. Ever.

I'm not against going though. In fact, I'd like to. But my best friend has five kids, and she's actually expecting her sixth with her new husband. I know she isn't going to be going rafting anytime soon.

While I'm happy for her, it makes me sad sometimes to be around her. Because she has a great marriage with my brother, the kind of marriage I'd like to have.

I watch her kids sometimes. I've also been spending a lot of time with my foster siblings. I like kids. You?

I'm glad things are working out with your app. Makes me happy to have helped.

How is your leg? Is it being too probing if I ask how you broke it?

Part of the reason I wanted to be a nurse was because I wanted to help people get better. Thanks for letting me know I've made you smile.

That made me smile.

I'm grateful too,

The Healing Pen

Chapter Five

$\mathcal{D}$ante stared at the letter in his hand, thinking.

Not about answering her. He could. There were no rules against what he was going to tell her about his leg. He didn't have to give details.

But just thinking. He'd seen the car accident as nothing but a bad thing.

He wasn't so sure anymore that was true. Funny how a little distance could shift a person's perspective.

"You're spacing out on me again. We need to talk about the minicamp."

"There's nothing to talk about." Dante looked at the Zoom app on his computer screen where his agent was speed walking on a treadmill. "I'm not in any shape to go. I talked to The Big Dude, and he knows where I'm at. He actually suggested I head out to some town his buddy preaches in, to get away for a little bit."

"Get away? Get away from what? All you've done is sit at your house and do nothing since the car accident. You need to start getting back in shape."

"I've been doing the upper body exercises prescribed to me

specifically by the team trainer," Dante said, careful not to let any of his irritation enter into his voice.

He had the best agent in the league in Dan Green. He definitely didn't want to lose him. Especially after the way his life had been going this year. He needed all the leverage he could get. Even with four years left on his contract.

Contracts didn't seem to mean anything anymore.

"And I've been working with my physical therapist on the lower body strength. The leg's mostly healed, I just want to make sure I'm smart with how I recondition."

"Yeah, yeah, I get that. But get away?"

"Maybe just get away from my head. I think that's what he's thinking. Who knows? The Big Dude doesn't always make sense, but usually whatever he has us doing works out."

Dan couldn't argue with that. "He's the best around. He really lucked out when you landed on his team."

Dante wasn't entirely sure it was luck, but he had to admit, because of Coach's unconventional approach to conditioning, which dovetailed beautifully with his own personal work ethic, he'd been able to excel, and most professionals agreed he was the best ever to play the tight end position in pro ball. He wouldn't mind leaving that as his legacy.

"My career would look a lot different with a different coach, for sure." He probably wouldn't have seen nearly the playing time, wouldn't have had whole plays designed around him and his strengths.

Just the thought made him long to throw some clothes in a shoulder bag and head out to the hill country where they always had minicamp at a small college in the hot Texas sun.

To see his buddies again.

Men weren't exactly known for their caring bedside manner, but he would have thought he'd have gotten more visits than what he had.

His quarterback and his running back had both been in several times, but his real lifeline through all of this had been The Healing Pen.

He supposed he owed her another thank you...it wouldn't be his first thank you, and she'd never accepted his apology.

Maybe he should say something about that. He was definitely feeling more comfortable with her, although because of the stipulations in place, he didn't really feel like he knew her.

Or maybe she didn't feel like she could open up to him. He hadn't exactly been welcoming.

She hadn't complained though. And she'd written back like clockwork. Six days after he sent a letter, he could expect one from her.

"As long as you know The Big Dude is good, and he knows you're gonna be hitting training camp in the best shape of your life." His agent continued to speed walk on the machine, but he checked his watch and looked up. "Got another call scheduled. Keep in touch with me."

Dante jerked his head and clicked out of the Zoom meeting.

He didn't want to talk about his lack of family or his miserable childhood, and he wasn't sure he could avoid that and still talk about how important football was to him.

How it had honestly saved his life, and that wasn't being dramatic.

How it had provided opportunities for him that he wouldn't have had otherwise, couldn't afford otherwise. How it had given him money and prestige and given him a name and a purpose and a life worth living, none of which he would have had if it hadn't been for football.

He owed the game everything.

He had a feeling The Healing Pen wouldn't understand. She didn't seem like a big sports person.

Interesting, how fading from the spotlight, even for just the time that he'd been off, had reduced his visibility in the romance department.

None of the girls he dated off and on again had stuck with him like The Healing Pen had.

It was partly his fault for not being on social media more, but he didn't want to depress himself by seeing everyone else's workouts when he couldn't.

It had truly surprised him how much of the attention he had gotten was not for him as a person but was because of his fame.

No, he definitely didn't want to mention football to The Healing Pen.

At least with her, he knew her attention wasn't because of his fame, nor because of what he was, definitely not because of who he was, but probably more because of the kind of person she was.

He didn't want her to change. He didn't want her to know that— at least before his accident—he had been one of the best players in pro football, and rich.

He liked the idea of someone liking him just for him and not for his fame or money or prestige.

He thought maybe he should treat her a little better than what he had.

Dear Healing Pen,

I don't think you're prying to ask how I broke my leg. It was a car accident. It happens to a lot of people. I was a passenger in one of my friend's cars. Funny how you look back in your life and you can see one decision that changed the direction of everything.

If this broken leg doesn't heal right, it could change my whole life.

Actually, some things I've been thinking about. First, I would have done anything to keep it from changing anything because I liked my life the way it was. But now, maybe with a little distance, a little perspective, I can see possibilities.

I'm the kind of person who works hard, sets a goal, and doesn't let anything distract him from it.

This broken leg was a distraction.

It's been kinda hard to handle.

I was talking to someone the other day, and I maybe realized that part of the reason that I haven't gone completely nuts is because of you. I figured I should thank you.

I also figured maybe I owe you a whitewater rafting trip. What do you think?

I also was thinking the people I thought would be around to see me haven't been. I'm disappointed about some of them, relieved about others, and a little annoyed at my stupidity for still more. I realize there were a lot of people who liked me not for me but for other things.

Regardless of why you're writing, you haven't left me, and I thought, maybe, we could be friends?

Your friend, hopefully,

Computer Geek

JOURNEE SAT on the grass beside the gently gurgling brook, in the middle of the meadow, along one of her favorite trails.

One of the best things about working in the ER was that she was able to work three- and four-day weeks, twelve-hour shifts, and then have an alternating three and four days off.

Which made it so she was able to spend time at her dad's cabin in the woods. The cabin was actually pretty fancy for a "cabin," but it was in some of the most beautiful country in the Ozarks, in Journee's opinion.

Not to mention there was a fun brook in the meadow that she was in now, plus lots of rocks to climb and places to explore.

When her parents had foster children, Journee often took them up for an overnight trip, and sometimes, they spent a couple nights, depending on the kids and how much they liked it.

Currently, her parents' latest charges, Frank and Darcy, were with her. Darcy was much more interested in horses, and Frank was a sports fanatic, but both of them were having fun wading in the brook, splashing and laughing, not far from where Journee sat with her notebook and with Computer Geek's latest letter.

She wasn't sure what exactly had caused his change of heart, but he seemed more vulnerable than he had in any other letter.

He said in a postscript he did run into a problem with his app and was working on it. But it also sounded like things were shifting in his professional life, whatever he did for a living.

She had to admit she was curious, and if it hadn't been for her promise to her dad, she'd be asking all kinds of questions.

She remembered her dad's warning though, and that was what prompted her hesitation.

She didn't really trust herself, but all of her heart and soul said to go for it. That, sure, like any other man in the world, he had hang-ups and problems, but she felt like she could trust him.

Maybe her feelings were wrong.

After all, she trusted Alex. That had been a mistake.

She couldn't live her life never trusting anyone again because she had made one bad decision.

The kids laughed, and she looked up in time to see Darcy slip, her arms fly around, and Frank reach out.

They helped each other, and both of them managed to stay on their feet. Barely.

The sight made her smile. She had a happy childhood thanks to Race and Penny adopting her.

She could go have a good time with Darcy and Frank, and maybe she wouldn't wait around for Mr. Right to have children. There were lots of kids who needed a home.

Although she wasn't sure what her life would be like, if she hadn't had a dad. Would she have been happy with just a mom?

She suspected, if that was all she knew, she'd have been happy with it.

She wasn't sure exactly whether she should go forward with that thought or not.

The Bible was clear that a man and a woman got together, and then they had children. But in a world that wasn't perfect, where there were children who needed a stable home, maybe a mom would be sufficient.

Or maybe the Lord would send a dad.

Setting aside her notebook, thinking a little more about Computer Geek and exactly how much she was going to open up to him, she yanked her shoes and socks off, rolled up her pant legs, and ran up the edge of the creek toward the children as she braced herself for the cold water.

Kids were only young once, and if she could make even one day in their childhood a special one, she wanted to do that.

Dear Computer Geek,

I would like to be your friend.

I understand what you're saying about people that you think will be there, and they're not.

I suppose we've all had people in our lives like that. It sounds like you maybe more than most.

I'd love to go whitewater rafting with you. I might be a big baby about it, though. I'm not big on fear.

While I think I would enjoy the rafting part of it, the whitewater I'm not so sure about.

I'm sorry to hear that you ran into trouble with your app. I hope you get the kinks worked out.

I know you said you didn't care for sheep, and I get your explanation. It made sense to me. What about gardening? I've actually been working on one this year and have really been enjoying it. Not necessarily because of eating what I grow, but because it's been fun to make the garden look pretty. I know, weird, right?

There's a festival in my town soon—like there are in July in towns across America. Everybody's gearing up for that now. It'll be here before we know it. Do you have plans for the summer?

I wanted to let you know, I think maybe writing to you has been as good for me as what you say it's been for you.

True, I wasn't stuck in the hospital necessarily, but I worked there. And thinking about your app, messing with it, has been a lot of fun. It's also made me think about how I treat people here under my care.

Like I said, you've been just as good for me. Maybe I should be the one thanking you.

I hope things are getting back to normal for you.

Your friend,

The Healing Pen

❄

Dear Healing Pen,

I've been getting the kinks worked out on my app. I need a little help, and so I looked a few things up online, got a little advice and some technical direction. Now it's just a matter of coding. Which I love. I can really geek out on that.

I'll save you the long-winded details.

Your comment on gardening piqued my interest.

Not necessarily because I care whether or not gardens look pretty, sorry, but because I have an interest in health. Which I assume as a nurse you probably do too. Maybe I should be more specific and say nutrition.

I guess what I'm saying is if you grow it and make it look pretty, I'll harvest it and turn it into something yummy. Cooking is a pastime of mine.

Not a passion, but when a guy lives by himself, he kind of has to learn how to feed himself, unless he can eat fast food all time. Which, considering my interest in nutrition, is really no option for me.

What do you grow? Seems like every garden needs to have tomatoes, and those are the basic ingredient for a lot of dishes. Healthy too. I guess I'm kind of weird, because I really like okra, and not fried. Most people don't. I'm not sure why. It's probably my favorite. That and radishes.

I understand radishes are easy to grow.

I've never actually grown anything, but I can see myself doing it.

I don't know if you got the same instructions I did, but I had to wait a year before I could tell you any details that might identify myself.

So maybe we can set up our whitewater rafting trip for next summer?

I suppose, since we're friends now, I'm not out of line to ask if you're married.

Don't worry, I'm not violating the terms of the pen pal agreement, I just want to know.

I'm not.

I'm not in a relationship either. I guess that was one of the things I was talking about when I said people didn't stick around.

Not that I was in a long-term relationship, but I kinda had a few girls who I considered more than friends.

I haven't talked to any of them more than three or four times since the accident.

I think they liked what I represented, or what I had, more than they liked me.

I was on social media a little bit last week; it looked like they'd all moved on. It made me feel dumb. But it didn't hurt. I wasn't really sad about it, so that probably says that I was just as invested in them as they were in me.

I hope I didn't scare you with all of that. I'm not trying to have a romance with you, just want you to know where I stand. I don't really believe in beating around the bush. It's always better to just come out and say things. Which reminds me, I'm going to be taking a trip in July and won't be able to write you while I'm gone.

DANTE STOPPED THERE and tapped his pencil on his desk. He debated back and forth about whether or not to tell The Healing Pen that he was going to Mistletoe, Arkansas.

Was that breaking the rules of the pen pal program?

From the way he understood it, thousands of people went to the Mistletoe festival.

But if she knew he would be there...maybe she'd go too and they wouldn't try to meet, but the idea that she was there, somewhere, would be kind of neat.

She didn't have to tell him that she was the kind of girl who didn't quit. Who persevered. Who started something and saw it through to the end.

He had a lot of those same characteristics, and he admired them in other people.

But maybe he didn't want to say anything to The Healing Pen because he didn't want her to be there. He didn't want to have to worry about her seeing him and being disappointed. Or seeing him and being awestruck by his name and his prestige in sports.

In other words, he didn't want her to be like the other girls who had left him when he was in the hospital and never really showed back up.

He wanted her to like him for him. The Computer Geek who was a little rough around the edges and had come from nothing.

Who knew what it was like to have literally nothing.

He considered not going to the festival in Mistletoe at all. But he didn't need The Big Dude to recommend that he do it for him to think it was a good idea.

He wasn't really big on Christmas, it had never been special in his childhood, wherever he was.

So it wasn't that he was necessarily interested in the Christmas aspect, but he supposed the small-town aspect was a draw. Also, The Big Dude seemed to have a lot of respect for the pastor that he knew there. Race Steiner.

All in all, it probably was a good idea.

He picked up his pen and started writing again.

I guess I asked you a bunch of personal questions, and of course, you don't have to answer anything that makes you uncomfortable. These are just things I know about all my other friends, and I figured I ought to know them about you. You can ask me anything you want too. I almost told you a bunch of stuff about myself, but I decided I didn't want to bore you.

If you ask, I'll answer.

I moved around a lot when I was a kid, but I have a memory of a really cool tree. Cool, because it was easy to climb, and I could get to the top without too much trouble. I spent a lot of time up on the top thinking about things. I suppose it's weird to have a boy that was as active as I was who also thought about stuff at the top of a tree.

In my experience, people are either thinkers or doers, but it's hard to find someone who does both.

Not that I'm special or anything, that's just one of the reasons I said I didn't really fit in.

Have to admit I'm kinda curious about you.

Your friend,

Computer Geek

Chapter Six

Dear Computer Geek,

Yes, we definitely found something we could do together. I love making a garden look good and love getting things to grow, and it would be wonderful to have someone to actually pick the stuff and do something with it.

And if you cook, I'm down for that.

I enjoy cooking too, though. Maybe we could do that together.

Hypothetically course.

I'm not married. And no, I don't think that was violating the terms of our pen pal agreement.

I don't have a boyfriend either. Once, a long time ago, there was someone, but I wasn't enough for him.

I'm sorry about your friends. I guess I'm using that word loosely, because it seems to me that when someone's in an accident, when they're in the hospital, when they're housebound, that's when they really need you to be there for them.

Maybe that's the nurse in me coming out though. I just see a lot of that. People in the hospital with no one visiting them. You know they have to have friends.

I guess, if you've never been there, you don't know how important it is to make time.

I'd say that maybe we should take a break from writing during your trip, but if you don't mind, I might write a note or two, just because I don't want to get out of the habit.

Isn't that the way it works?

I'll quit writing because you're on a trip, and you don't write because you're gone, and then we just never start again.

I won't if you don't want me to, though.

I told you before, I don't have any trouble having a conversation with myself. I can write it down on paper and send it to you.

It's kind of hard to joke on paper, but that was a joke.

Do you like to laugh?

Laughing,

The Healing Pen

Dear Healing Pen,

One boyfriend? That's it?

Really?

Sorry. I honestly don't know anybody like that. Hard for me to even imagine that.

I guess you better talk about something else, because I don't want you to ask me how many girlfriends I've had. I'm honestly not sure I could tell you a number. Not sure what counts as a girlfriend anyway. The girls I was seeing before my accident—and yes, that was plural—well, I'm not sure they count as girlfriends or not.

That's really a conversation I don't want to have.

I guess we just had it though, didn't we?

Your other question...do I like to laugh?

Is there anyone who would say no to that? I sure wouldn't.

There's a lot of people who might be surprised at that because I am pretty serious and driven. Having the accident maybe made me see that. I wouldn't have called myself serious necessarily before that.

Driven, yes, I've always been driven. But I kind of have excuses for it. Reasons I feel like I do. You know, your childhood shapes you. And I wanted to make something out of my life. And I knew that if that was going to happen, I was going to have to work for it, because no one was going to hand me anything. I was a pretty scrappy kid, in case you didn't notice.

I guess I'm a pretty scrappy adult too.

I hope you can be friends with a scrappy fella.

So how's our garden growing? And yeah, as I wrote that, I was thinking your name must be Mary. Mary, Mary, quite contrary, how does your garden grow?

I guess I can't really call it our garden if I'm not helping you.

Next year.

So, I know you like gardens and water and you only had one boyfriend.

Tell me something more.

Friends talk to each other,

Computer Geek

Dear Computer Geek,

I can't believe you're giving me a hard time for only having one boyfriend.

Isn't it a lot less normal for you to have girls that you're not even sure whether you can call them your girlfriends or not?

Is that the way people do things nowadays?

I'm seriously asking that question too. I live in a small town. I'm not the only one who's only ever had one boyfriend.

My sister has never had a boyfriend. She's too wrapped up in her horses to even notice that there is such a thing as boys.

I think she's kind of intimidating to guys too. She's pretty competitive, and everything she tries, she's extremely successful.

Although her best friend is a boy. Really, he's her best friend like a friend, friend. The kind of friends that you and I are. I don't think that they realize that boys and girls do things other than work together and goof off together.

It's funny, I can't use her name, but my sister and I are so different, yet we get along really well. Sometimes, I think opposites attract because they complement each other.

Haven't figured out whether you and I are opposites yet.

So there, you know I have a sister. I also like ice cream.

And I like to laugh. Like everyone, I guess. Although, I almost want to disagree with you on that. I've met more than one person who acts like laughing is sin.

Eating ice cream and laughing,
The Healing Pen

Dear Healing Pen,
Everyone likes ice cream.

I'm digging, because I know there are things about you that are really neat and cool and unique, and I want to know them. Every time you give me one of those things—you like laughing, you like ice cream—it just makes me want to dig harder until I find out those things—the unique things that make you special—I know are there.

I'm guessing you like chocolate too. Since everyone does, except me.

I'm a fruit guy. I suppose in more ways in one. (That was a joke. I guess it's not much of a joke if I have to point it out to you, is it?)

What's your favorite vegetable? Although, I suppose just because you garden doesn't mean you like vegetables. Especially since you're doing it for looks.

Do you grow houseplants? Maybe you've painted the walls in your room purple?

Do you wear sandals in the winter?

Maybe you have a beard? (I know that it's shallow for me to care how you look, and honestly, I mostly don't. I'm not sure how I feel about a beard though. On you. I actually do have a beard. I've been told girls like beards. I suppose that's why I have one. Because I don't really give a flip whether I have hair on my face or not, although hair is easier since then I don't have to shave.)

All right, I want to know about you, and I end up talking about myself. The next letter you send better have a bunch of personal stuff in it so you can satisfy my curiosity.

Waiting impatiently,

Computer Geek

PS. I'm going to email you a link for the app prototype. I think you're going to be pleasantly impressed. If you're not, break it to me gently. I'm kind of proud of this.

Dear Computer Geek,

For the first time since I met you, I was tempted to email you. I wanted to tell you how very, very impressed I was with your app. I almost couldn't wait for my turn to write. Snail mail is no joke.

I know you said you had some help, but I got the

feeling that it was informational help, and so I'm thinking you did this all yourself. I'm super impressed. I'm not lying.

What happens now?

Wow. You're pretty demanding. I guess I'm glad I found this out now before our casual friendship deepened into close friends.

I'm kidding. Sorry. I think if we were talking, I'd be able to see your sense of humor better, and you mine.

Anyway, you asked me specifically about my favorite vegetable. I'm always a little sketchy about what constitutes a vegetable. Seriously. Because I like tomatoes, but tomatoes are a fruit. So are pumpkins.

And I think, technically, radishes are a root.

I'm not sure they qualify as a vegetable. But if we're just including everything that you typically grow in a garden and calling it all vegetables, my favorite is spinach—cooked with butter and maybe a little garlic. And not cook cooked, just heated enough that the leaves are wilted. And it's hot enough to melt the butter.

There's nothing better.

In gardening, there are also not too many things that are harder because it takes so much raw spinach to make even one helping of cooked.

Maybe peas are harder. It takes a lot of work to get enough peas for one person to eat. Let alone to put on the table for a family.

I like spinach in everything. I also like cheese in

everything. And garlic makes everything better too. Not to mention, it's good for your health. Along with honey.

If I could do something really radical, I would like to have a beehive.

Pretty out there, isn't it?

Are we still friends?

You know, you kinda have to stick with me. With the bees and everything. After all, you admitted you had more girlfriends than you could count, and you weren't even sure how to count them. And I stuck with you. Just wanted to point that out. In case the bees were off-putting.

So there, that's unique, isn't it?

I can't really think of anything else. I'm pretty boring. In fact, I think you'd be hard-pressed to find someone who is less exciting than me.

Not unique,
The Healing Pen

Dear Healing Pen,

I think you're far from boring. I think you're right about the vegetables too. I happened to be making a grocery run on the day your letter came. I may or may not have been sitting in the driveway waiting for the mailman to deliver it before I left for my trip. And I may or may not have sat in my driveway after the mailman left, opened your letter, and read it before I went shopping.

You can read that however you want to.

I like the bee idea. I think I can get into that too. I like honey anyway. So no, you're definitely not weird, and yeah, I definitely want to be friends.

Anyway, I added spinach to my grocery list, along with garlic. I already had butter.

It occurred to me when I got to the store and was looking at the vegetables that spinach grown in the garden might taste different than spinach grown in a grocery store.

(That was a joke.)

Strawberries at the U pick are much better than strawberries that you get in the store—the ones that came from California. Not that I have anything against California, but I assume that strawberries that have to travel across the country are bred for hardiness and not taste.

While strawberries you get from the U pick are bred for taste. I know that because one of my girlfriends (those numberless things that I've had in the past) dragged me to the U pick and made me pick strawberries. She called it a date.

At the time, I did not appreciate it.

That was probably eight years ago.

Isn't it funny how much wiser we feel after eight years of life goes by?

Think I might actually enjoy a "date" like that at this point in my life.

Back then, I was definitely not impressed.

She wasn't my girlfriend very long.

Actually, no one has ever been my girlfriend for very long. I can get 'em, but I just can't keep 'em.

Up until not that long ago, I pretty much blamed the girls.

I'm rethinking that.

In fact, I've rethunk it. (Is rethunk a word?)

It's me.

It was me anyway.

I know you're not going to see the connection between you and what I figured out, but I figured out I was selfish. I still am, because this isn't the kind of thing that you get rid of overnight. But I see why I had a lot of girlfriends and never anything deep.

I'm not entirely sure what to do about it.

So I want to hear more about your boyfriend. Your one, single, lone boyfriend. How long did that last?

Waiting on answers,

Computer Geek

PS. Really says something when I was more interested in finding out about your boyfriend than I was in telling you about my app. It's really consumed most of my waking hours. I have something else that I'm working on, that I have to work on, but after that, it's been all computer app. I've got a team on it now. They'll take care of all the details. I've got a really good feeling this is going to take off.

You know half the profits are yours. After all, there wouldn't be an app if you hadn't suggested it.

Chapter Seven

Dear Computer Geek,

I guess I'm just the opposite. My boyfriend was my boyfriend for six years.

He was my high school sweetheart. We did everything together. I thought we were going to spend our lives together. I couldn't picture myself with anyone else. I was pretty devastated when it didn't work out. I'd invested everything I had into it. I'm never going to do that again.

My mom used to make something with spinach and cheese and cut them into squares. She made them for holidays, and I love them.

She made them just for me because no one else in our family liked them.

I would eat spinach in anything though. Filling balls. Spinach and vegetable soup. Turkey noodle soup is better with spinach in it too. Spinach on pizza. Spinach in hoagies, and I'm not kidding about that. In fact, spinach is the one thing I don't joke about.

Do you like mushrooms?

I know they're not a vegetable, but I think they're good.

I know that's kind of a black-or-white question. I don't know people who kinda like mushrooms. You either love them or you hate them. Like nurses.

There's a lot of things like that. Black and white. Love or hate.

But I think there's even more things where there's a gray area.

To me, that's probably where you're at in crediting me with showing you that maybe some of the fault in your relationship was you.

I don't really believe it. We never talked about that. I never said anything.

But I'm glad you saw it. Not that I think you're right. I don't know.

But from experience, looking at myself, I know I'm definitely more selfish than I want to be. Embarrassingly selfish. I was just having a debate with myself about something that I know I need to do, and it's not that I don't want to, it's just I know it's a big sacrifice, and I think that if I do it, it could make it so that I don't get what I want, although it would be giving other people what they wanted.

I know I'm being vague. I have to be. I don't

want to give any identifying details. And break the agreement.

Just know, being selfish is common. And I'm afflicted as well.

Also, our friendship does not require that you split your profits with me.

An idea is just an idea, nothing you can touch or hold in your hand, not until someone takes it and makes it into something. That's what you did. You did the hard work. I just threw something out and wrote about it to you.

It was a nice thought though.

Keep my royalties. Maybe you can use them to pay for a whitewater rafting trip. Don't think I'm going to forget about that.

So, you've asked some personal things, and in the spirit of our friendship, I'm curious about something.

How many girlfriends is too many to count?

I'm sorry if that's too personal.

I'm waiting too,

The Healing Pen

Dear Healing Pen,

When I say too many to count, I mean it. I generally think that was part of my problem.

I'm not sure how to explain it. Maybe it's like going to eat at a buffet. You look at all the really good dishes and maybe all the desserts, and you just can't make up your mind. I always end up getting more than I can eat, because I want everything.

I guess maybe that was the way I was with girls. I looked at them and didn't want to settle with just one. There were too many that looked interesting to me.

I know, that's probably hard for someone like you to understand. Someone that's really happy with just one guy. At least you sounded like you were happy with him.

I don't know. Maybe it's also a prestige thing.

To some extent, the girl on my arm gave me a certain feeling. Maybe the way a fancy car or fancy watch or an expensive suit might. It all makes you feel like you've arrived. It doesn't make me look good, but I guess girls were objects.

That really makes me seem shallow to admit that, but that's not uncommon. Not among men anyway. You look at the girl beside you, and you judge how people are looking at you based on how she looks.

It has nothing to do with her personality or who she is. But everything to do with what she looks like, and maybe a little about what she's achieved.

If she's a big-name actress or someone on social media that everybody recognizes, people might look at me and think I must really be something, to have a car like that and a watch like that and a suit like that and a girl like that.

Man, I'm embarrassed to explain it. That's the way almost every guy I know thinks.

The guys around me aren't really normal though.

And just for the record, I don't think like that anymore. I guess it's been kind of a while since I felt like that, but I knew I needed to be like that.

Peer pressure for sure.

I know. I was a little too honest. Honestly, I'd rather talk about bees and spinach.

And my app. It's almost ready to launch.

I hope you write back soon, maybe sooner than you usually do? I'm kind of nervous to mail this thinking you probably aren't going to talk to me again.

Anxious,

Computer Geek

Dear Computer Geek,

I wrote the same day I received your letter. Normally I don't, but I wanted to assure you that the way you treat your girlfriends doesn't affect how much I like you and whether or not we're friends.

Maybe that seems odd, and I can't say that I approve of what you explained, but so far at least, you haven't treated me like that. And I suppose, even if you do, I might not be successful, but I would try to live out the principle that you don't treat others the way they treat you, you treat them the way you want to be treated.

Now, I'll be the first person to admit it's a lot easier to live that out when people are being nice to you.

It's a real struggle, and I'm not very successful, when people are being unkind.

In fact, there's actually prevalent teaching even in the church today that says you have to distance yourself from toxic relationships.

And that you're a doormat if you allow people to be unkind to you.

I guess Jesus was the great doormat. After all, Calvary is the epitome of allowing people to be unkind to you, isn't it?

That thought always reminds me of the song about how he could have called ten thousand angels, not just to get him off the cross but to strike everyone dead who wanted him there.

I suppose that would have been modern psychology in action.

I'm pretty happy Jesus doesn't subscribe to modern psychology.

He's supposed to be our example.

Sorry, you hit a nerve. Obviously.

Anyway, I guess I don't need to beat that horse to death anymore.

I think this is the last letter you'll get before you leave on your trip.

You never said whether or not you mind if I write even though you can't answer me.

I told you I don't have any trouble answering myself. I have whole conversations with myself in my head.

Now, I'm going to be worried as to whether or not we're still friends.

That's not really something I could admit to normal people.

There, you wanted me to tell you what makes me

unique.

Is unique synonymous with crazy?
In uniqueness (craziness),
The Healing Pen

Dear Healing Pen,

Unique is not synonymous with crazy.

I've heard people say it's okay to talk to yourself as long as you don't answer yourself, but I don't see any reason why you can't answer yourself. What's the point if you don't?

I've never actually tried that. I don't usually talk to myself. I could see me talking to a dog, though.

I've thought about getting one. Do you have a dog?

They don't eat vegetables, so I wouldn't have competition there. Although, I have to admit I do like red meat. I suppose a dog and I might have some issues over that.

Regardless, I think talking to a dog is more socially acceptable than talking to yourself. Just out of curiosity, and this is a serious question, do you do it out loud? I mean answer yourself out loud.

I promise your answer won't go any further.

I told you I was going on a trip, but I didn't mention that after I get back from the trip, I'm actually going to be starting my job. It's going to be pretty consuming. It kinda makes me wish that I could tell you what it is, so maybe you'd understand a little better. I'll still be able to write, but I'll be busy.

I know your job is hard and stressful at times. I guess mine is too.

Anyway, I just wanted to warn you. I wasn't kidding about waiting at the mailbox for your letters. You've never really said anything about mine, so maybe it won't matter to you if they're not quite as clockwork as they have been.

I guess we can cross that bridge when we come to it.

What are you doing with the rest of your summer?

I'll talk to you when I get back from my trip.

I'm interested to see what kind of letters you write to yourself while I am gone.

I appreciate your sense of humor.

I wanted to say I appreciated what you said to me about doing unto others.

I hope I'm not out of line with this: you're the most interesting person I've ever met.

Yours truly,

Computer Geek

Chapter Eight

$\mathcal{A}$s Dante walked down the street of Mistletoe, he was struck by how much the town felt like home.

Not that he ever really had a home. But as he traveled the country playing in different cities, he'd seen a lot of different places.

Born in Michigan, he went to college in California before landing in Galveston and spending his entire professional career there.

Nothing had prepared him for the small-town, down-home, welcoming feel of Mistletoe.

Even if it was all decked out for Christmas in the middle of July.

That actually gave it an even cuter vibe.

Not that he'd ever been into cute vibes.

He supposed his pen pal had a little to do with his new perspective on life.

Funny how meeting someone who wasn't quite the same as you had a tendency to shift the way you thought about things.

It had for him anyway.

He'd been in a football bubble all his life. Everything revolved around the game.

It still did, but having a friend outside of his normal

"friendships" had given him a different perspective. Not that his core beliefs had necessarily changed, just that he realized that everything he had always assumed wasn't necessarily everything the rest of the world assumed.

His assumptions, and things he felt to be absolutely true, and things he had never understood how other people could think or believe had changed, and he realized that maybe other people were just as justified in their beliefs as he was.

Maybe it was as much the accident that he'd had, where he faced a world that might not involve playing football for the first time in his life, as it was writing to The Healing Pen.

She was in a town like this somewhere in Arkansas.

The thought caused a small hurricane of sensation to skip through his chest.

He wanted to meet her.

And he didn't want to meet her.

Pulling open the door to the diner, he started to walk in. He was supposed to meet Pastor Race Steiner here, at two o'clock.

Dante was five minutes early.

He almost ran into a woman in scrubs who was waiting for him to go in before going out the door.

Scrubs. Could this be The Healing Pen?

Then he noticed she held the hand of a little boy and a little girl in each of hers, and he dismissed the idea. It was way too coincidental that he'd be coming to the same town she was in. Plus, The Healing Pen had never said anything about having children.

Of course, he hadn't exactly asked. He'd been more interested in whether or not she had a husband or boyfriend.

It was kind of embarrassing to admit now, because he'd been pretty obvious with his questions. He'd been interested.

He was still interested.

Of course, a person could hide a lot in written correspondence. But that didn't mean he didn't want to see if there couldn't be something between them.

She was different than all the other girls he knew. More of that getting out of his own circle and finding out that there were things in the world that he hadn't experienced.

He could understand why men would stick with just one woman if they had a woman like The Healing Pen.

Had she ever said why she broke up with her high school sweetheart? He didn't think she had, and he hadn't asked.

When he wrote to her, he had too many things he wanted to say and none that were appropriate.

Young and pretty, with sparkling green eyes and dark, almost black hair, the woman who came out of the diner hardly looked old enough to be the children's mother.

She looked up at him and gave him a smile that showcased a deep dimple in one cheek and made her eyes crinkle.

"Hey there. Welcome to Mistletoe," she said, her voice husky and sweet with a thread of humor in it that tugged a little at his heart.

"Thanks. It's a unique town from what I've seen so far," he said, more words than he might normally have said to a stranger. Especially a woman.

He probably would have nodded his head and walked on by. Just because in his experience, women knew who he was and wanted to use him as the arm candy he had explained to The Healing Pen he used women for.

He had always wanted to do the choosing. He didn't want to be chosen.

It wasn't hard to shake that off, whether it was the town atmosphere, or whether it was the woman who walked by him.

"I hope you're staying for the festival. It's definitely unique, although Mistletoe does Christmas year-round." The woman's smile was friendly, and there was no glimmer of recognition in her eyes.

"Do you work in the ER?" he asked, unable to clamp his lips shut around the question.

The little boy was swinging her hand, and he could see there was no ring on it. It made him feel like the pull she had on him was okay, like the odds that she could be The Healing Pen weren't crazy impossible.

Her brows drew together, and she seemed confused. Her mouth opened, but before she could say anything, a man's voice said, "You have to be Dante."

Dante glanced up, having been so focused on the woman he hadn't realized there was a man behind her.

"I am."

"I'm Pastor Race. And that's my daughter, Journee, and two of my other children, Frank and Darcy."

"Actually, I hadn't gotten around to introducing myself to Journee," Dante said, his eyes back on the woman who was smiling again. "It's good to meet you, Journee."

Maybe he just hadn't gotten out enough lately.

He walked without a limp, and even though his leg gave him twinges of pain at times, it was probably as healed up as it was going to be.

He'd stepped up his workouts and had a Skype call scheduled with his trainer for later in the day.

"It's good to meet you too, Dante. Maybe we'll see each other around later," the woman said as the children pulled her off, saying something about a pond and ducks, and she turned and allowed them to lead her down the sidewalk.

Of course, she wasn't The Healing Pen. Although she could be a nurse. That's what the scrubs said anyway. Or doctor. Or therapist.

The Healing Pen hadn't said anything about her father being a pastor.

He turned back to Race and grabbed his hand, shaking it. "Thank you so much for meeting with me. Coach Samuels has the highest respect for you, and he seemed to think the trip to Mistletoe was just what I needed."

"Sometimes, getting out and getting a new perspective is helpful. Your coach talks very highly about you and your work ethic and your ability to inspire the men under you to work to their fullest potential," Pastor Race said as he led the way into the diner and chose a corner booth.

At this time in the afternoon, it was pretty quiet.

"Those are high words of praise coming from Coach Samuels," Dante said, and he meant it. Coach didn't use a lot of lavish praise, so the words he did say carried a lot of weight.

The compliment squeezed up his neck and made him feel good.

"Coach had some good words of praise for you, too. He said I could learn a lot from you. And I think he knew I needed to get out before camp started."

"I agree. Coach Samuels has been in it for a lot of years. He understands his players."

"That's true."

"How has the pen pal thing been going? That's actually how Coach Samuels and I started talking about you. He'd heard about our program and thought you would be a good candidate."

"Something else Coach was right about, I guess. I feel like I've learned a lot and had my eyes opened a lot of ways. At first, the restrictions on not being allowed to share any personal details felt restrictive and maybe even overkill, but it almost forced us to talk about ideas rather than things in a way, and that actually has been really helpful to me. I hope that the person I'm corresponding with feels the same." Dante fingered the menu the waitress had set down with a smile after taking their drink orders and walking away.

Christmas music played softly in the background, which didn't totally shock him, as the Christmas tree in the corner decorated with little American flags didn't either.

There was another tree in the opposite corner that was decorated like an actual Christmas tree at Christmastime, and Dante wondered idly if that was because of the festival coming up, or if that's the way it always was around here.

He had a feeling it was the latter.

"In almost every instance. The program has been very popular,"

Pastor Race said with a little smile, maybe a bit of humble pride if there was such a thing.

"Glad to hear it."

They didn't say anything while the waitress set their drinks down and took their orders. Dante ordered a burger and fries, although as he ordered he was kind of thinking to himself about vegetables and wondered if it would be too weird if he asked about the best gardens in town.

If this was her town—the odds were high that it was not—that would probably be obvious. He wasn't supposed to be finding out who The Healing Pen was, and while he really did want to know, he felt like he needed to respect the parameters that Pastor Race had set up.

So far, they'd been working. In a little over half a year, he could ask personal questions. That wouldn't be too long to wait, and it would actually be a good idea since he would be consumed with football during football season and wouldn't really have time to give The Healing Pen the attention she deserved if she was even as interested in him as he was in her.

"I wanted to thank you for the advice you'd given when I was in the hospital before I started on the pen pal program. I was, as Coach suspected, falling into the trap of questioning why God would allow an accident like that happen and why was it me that had to go through the extra rehabilitation and pain and all the work required in recovering. It seems like with my childhood and background, God had already given me enough."

"I'm glad you found my advice helpful. Sometimes, we just close ourselves off to the possibilities that God might be opening in front of us."

"That's exactly what was happening. I'm still not sure that I want to give up football, but it doesn't look like I have to. It just looks like it was another trial to go through."

"Sometimes, God opens doors through these trials." Maybe

Pastor Race was hinting at something, although as Dante squirted ketchup on his plate, he wasn't sure exactly what that was.

"I know." Maybe the door that was opening had to do with The Healing Pen. He could only hope so. Maybe the accident would be worth it, if he found a woman who liked him for more than what he did on the field.

Thinking of that, maybe he didn't want to meet The Healing Pen at all, and he hoped this actually *wasn't* her town. Because if he did, she'd find out who he was. He definitely didn't want that. Not until he knew her better.

They talked a little more about some of the things Race had given him advice about—God's plan and trials. He sounded so much like The Healing Pen it was almost uncanny.

He just had a couple bites of his sandwich hamburger and a few odd fries left when Race steepled his hands and set his chin on his fingers.

"You know we're going to have a Christmas festival here in Mistletoe, and you're staying for it, correct?"

"For a few days. Yes."

"Good. I think you'll enjoy it, and it will be fun and relaxing." Race paused. "I was wondering if you'd be interested in participating. I have a few contests that have slots that haven't been filled. I know you're used to performing in front of people."

"Playing football is a little different than participating in a small-town contest," Dante said with a small grin.

The thought didn't exactly strike fear into his heart, but it didn't exactly make him eager to get up in front of a bunch of strangers and do something weird.

"You're not going to ask me to swallow knives or walk on hot coals, are you?"

Pastor Race laughed. "Of course not. It's a Christmas contest. You swallow Christmas ornaments and walk on burning trees."

"That makes a world of difference."

"I'm kidding. I have an odd request, then I have a serious

request." He pulled a notepad out of his paper pocket. "First, the serious request. Don't feel you have to. But this seemed like a good thing for you to do. I thought maybe the townspeople would get a kick out of it. We have a Not Such an Ironman Ironman Contest, Christmas style, of course."

"Not Such an Ironman?"

"That's right. It's kind of an obstacle course and one of our more popular contests for spectators. You'd be paired up with someone, and instead of running for so many miles or biking and swimming, you do Christmas activities throughout the course. You're timed, of course, and judges will judge you as well. I just need one more person to complete a pair, and there'll be five couples competing."

"Exactly what do we have to do?"

"Nothing too hard. It changes from year to year. Things like build a gingerbread house together, decorate a tree, climb up the chimney, which is probably the most difficult for many of the contestants, but I don't think you'll have a problem with it, and make a pumpkin pie. Wrap a present. That type of thing. I'm not even sure if they have the whole contest together yet. My wife is usually in charge of it, and she's been a little busy with the kids we're fostering."

"I see. Sure." He shrugged his shoulders. "I'll do it."

It didn't sound like anything he'd be totally comfortable doing, but it did sound like fun, and it actually kind of made him feel included in the town to be participating in the festival. Almost like he was a local.

"I'm really curious to find out what the strange request is. Because that didn't sound too normal to me."

Pastor Race laughed. "Well, this is actually a personal favor. And I'm thinking that if all goes well, you'll end up not having to participate. I just need you to be willing." Race gave him a look that made his insides shiver in fear. Which, considering that he was used to staring down a couple hundred pound defensive lineman eyeballing him on the line of scrimmage, really said something.

"Okay?"

"I am hoping that my daughter and her best friend will be in the kissing contest together. However, instead of asking them directly, since my daughter is a little bit contrary, nothing rebellious—" He put his hand up as though warding off any interruption that Dante might make. "—but sometimes people just need a little nudge."

He lifted a brow, as though thinking about Dante's accident as a little nudge.

"Not that I'm playing God, but sometimes, a parent's perspective is a little different than their children's perspective, and sometimes, the things I try don't work. But, I'm not sure if Coach told you, I used to be a cardiac surgeon. Seems like I've graduated from that to actual emotional matters of the heart. With my children as my primary studies."

"No. He didn't tell me. Should I be calling you Dr. Steiner?"

"Pastor Race is fine. I retired a long time ago. And some days, I miss it. At times, being a cardiac surgeon was a lot less pressure than being a pastor, if you can believe it."

Dante gave a nod. "I don't have any trouble believing that. I'd rather operate on someone's heart than mess with anyone's feelings."

He and Race nodded together, totally on the same page.

"Anyway, there's a kissing contest, and I was wondering if you would partner or agree to partner with Blakely. I'm expecting you to not have to actually enter the contest. I think when she hears that I'm asking her to partner with a football player, she'll go to her best friend and ask him to partner with her. That's my expectation."

"A football player specifically? Is there a problem with football players around here?"

"No. Not around here. Blakely has a thing. I don't know, I've never really been able to explain it. Sometimes, I just think about it the way some people are afraid of bats, and other people don't like loud noises, and some people have claustrophobia." He shrugged. "I'm not a psychologist. But she's just never liked sports players and especially football players. I really don't know why."

"Hmm. I wonder if I should be offended over this?"

"Probably. You could be offended for the entire pro football association, college players, high school players, and right down to peewee. Everyone should be offended. Because there's no logic behind her aversion. I don't think you need to take it personally though, because as a person, she'll love you. She just prefers cowboys over ballplayers, I guess. Maybe I should explain she's always been into horses, and she barrel raced for a while, but trick riding is where her passion is."

"I take it her best friend must be a cowboy?"

Race grinned. "Good guess. He's a rodeo guy. And they're perfect for each other. They just don't see it. I'm kind of hoping that'll change if they enter the kissing contest together."

"All right. I guess if she doesn't back out, I can give her a peck on the cheek."

"I like the way you think."

Dante grinned but cowered a little inside. He'd kissed women he'd only known for an evening, blind dates, and women he'd asked out, barely knowing them. He'd done far more than just peck them on the cheek, so it wasn't really a hardship exactly, except his thoughts along those lines had changed some since writing to The Healing Pen.

He had a feeling that kissing meant a little more to her than it ever had to him.

He kinda liked the idea of making it special.

He doubted he could get her to talk to him about her ideas on kissing though. How exactly would he be able to bring up that subject without being completely obvious?

He grinned at the thought.

Chapter Nine

On the day before Mistletoe's Christmas in July festival was supposed to start, Journee spent the morning with Darcy and Frank, helping her mother make two hundred gingerbread men for the decorating contest, setting up tables along the entire stretch of Main Street, and hanging up more red ribbons than she could count.

She didn't have a chance to grab lunch until after three that afternoon. She took her sandwich and her current notebook and snuck up to the hayloft in the animal shed. The men were still working on getting the portable pens set up and unloading animals, but it would be quiet and she would be alone up in the loft.

She finished her sandwich and was engrossed in her writing when her sister Blakely scurried up the ladder and intruded upon her solitude.

Crawling over, Blakely came to the end of the stack of hay bales that were probably there from last year and just about jumped out of her skin to see Journee sitting there.

"Holy smokes. You scared me to death." Blakely sat back on her haunches and glared at her. "What are you doing here?"

"It's obvious, isn't it?" Journee said, closing the notebook, not wanting Blakely to be looking over her shoulder as she wrote. Not that she was writing anything to Computer Geek that wasn't proper. It was just private.

"No?" Blakely said.

"What are you doing up here?" Journee asked, wanting to change the subject.

"I'm hiding from him." Blakely jerked her chin in the direction of the guys. They were too far under the edge of the loft for Journee to see them, but their voices carried up clearly.

"You're hiding from Martin?" Journee asked, her face scrunched up, and her head tilted.

"No, silly." Although that was who had been speaking. "From the football player."

Journee's lips canted up, and she grinned knowingly. Blakely's aversion to sports figures and ballplayers in particular was no secret in their town. She thought maybe it had to do with cowboys being the "real" sportspeople in Blakely's eyes, although they'd never really talked about it.

Blakely rolled over to the edge of the loft, peering down. She lay there for a minute as though looking for something. Journee took that time to put her garbage in her bag and finish the sentence she'd been writing.

She'd barely gotten it done before Blakely scrambled back, dropping her head immediately, looking embarrassed.

"I take it from the way you're acting that someone saw you," Journee said, muted humor in her voice.

"Yeah. Martin was laughing at me, and the football player happened to look up. And there I was." She sat up and brushed her front off, crossing her legs and giving Journee a sincere look. Leaning forward, she put her hand on her knee. "I did need to talk to you. And it looks like you have some time?"

Journee laughed a little and rolled her eyes. "You're up here. You might as well tell me whatever it was that you wanted to tell me."

"I need advice."

"I thought the younger sister was supposed to get advice from the older sister?"

"Forget all that. This is important."

"What do you need?"

Blakely explained that Martin had agreed to be her partner in the kissing contest so she didn't have to be partnered with the football player. "But you can see that Martin and I don't want to win."

Journee remembered the shiver of excitement that had travelled up her spine when she'd met Dante at the diner. There was a part of her that said she wouldn't mind being paired in a kissing contest with him. But she understood Blakely's aversion.

"Yeah. Whoever wins gets badgered constantly to kiss for the next hundred years at least. Unless you break up and marry other people, and then you still might get begged to kiss. There are no guarantees in a small town."

"Exactly. So Martin and I don't want to win. But neither one of us has ever watched the kissing contest."

"You're missing out. You can learn a lot of things from the kissing contest."

"Well, I guess we'll get to learn this year, but we need to know, what do winners do? We need to make sure we don't do that."

Journee eyed her. Blakely truly had no idea that she and Martin were perfect together. It wouldn't surprise her at all if her dad had somehow finagled the situation so that they would actually kiss and figure out that they were meant to be together.

Journee might be able to help with that...

Blakely tapped her fingers on her leg, waiting. Finally, she couldn't stand the silence of her sister any longer. "I was thinking if we just act awkward. You know, like turn our heads the same way, miss our mouths, giggle... What else?"

"You haven't kissed too many people, have you?"

"That has nothing to do with this."

"I'm not saying that's a bad thing, I'm just saying awkwardness is kinda cute in a first kiss especially. The audience will love it, and the judges will score high. I mean, it's not like a super romantic Hollywood kiss, but it's perfect for small towns. Awkwardness, giggling, fumbling a little. People love it."

Blakely looked stunned. Journee tried not to smile. Maybe Blakely and Martin would have a real first kiss after all. "Okay. So we have to pretend that we're old hands at kissing." She grimaced. "That might be hard."

"That's what I was thinking. No one's gonna believe that you and Martin all the sudden want to kiss each other, and have been for a long time, unless you guys act like you're already together." Journee was kind of proud of her serious tone and expression, despite the fact that she really wanted to giggle.

"You think we should? Should we be like holding hands or something so people think that we're actually a couple? Because I can kinda see your point. Kissing probably gets boring after you've been with someone for a while."

"Maybe you should spend a little less time with your horses and a little more time figuring out how to live life."

"You're a good one to talk. Other than Alex, who doesn't really count, you've never had a boyfriend."

"Maybe Alex was enough." She didn't want to talk about Alex. Actually hadn't thought of him in a really long time. Computer Geek had kind of taken over that real estate in her brain. She still wasn't thinking she wanted to get into another relationship, but she definitely didn't mind dreaming about Computer Geek as long as he stayed in his area of the country and she in hers.

She didn't want to meet him and ruin all her beautiful daydreams.

"I'll give you that," Blakely finally said. Journee was thankful she didn't press the issue. She didn't want to talk to anyone about Computer Geek. "The kissing contest is tomorrow. Do you think we have enough time to act like we're a couple?"

"Will Martin even go along with it?"

Blakely bit her lip and twisted a straw stem in her hand. "I think so. Our parents are actually pushing Krissy at him, and he and I have an agreement. I think he'd be willing to do this to make it look legit."

"He helps you, and you help him?" Journee said, and there might have been just a trace of envy in her voice. She definitely wished she had a best friend who would do the same for her.

"I'm pretty blessed to have Martin," Blakely said, responding to the tone of her voice and not the words. Yeah, definitely envy in there.

"You are. I think maybe neither one of you know exactly what you have," she said thoughtfully, running her finger down the spirals of her notebook and not looking at Blakely while she said it.

"You might be right about that," Blakely said slowly, like she was thinking about her friendship and realizing she needed to appreciate it. "I'm pretty sure he'll go along with it. Do you think it will work?"

"I don't think you need to be obvious about it. Just let him put his arm around you. The rumor mill will pick it up and take it from there. You know how rumors travel in a small town. All you and Martin need to do is hold hands, and the whole town's going to have you married by next Friday."

Blakely grunted. "True."

"I know."

"Now about the kind of kiss that we need to have. You said awkward was a winning attribute. What's a losing attribute?"

"Disinterest?" Journee said, scrunching her brows up, her finger going to her cheek as she pretended to give the question serious thought. "Or, I don't know, there's just no spark. Boring. Like you've done it a million times and you don't really care about the person you're kissing. I think those kisses are the ones that are forgettable and that nobody votes for." She highly doubted if Blakely and Martin actually got into a kiss that it would be boring, but she wasn't going to tell Blakely that.

"Nobody votes for? I thought there were judges?"

"There are, but they also get audience participation. It varies from year to year, and the judges' scores are weighted heavily, but typically, they take opinions from the audience. But every year, it's been different. The kissing contest is kind of eccentric, which is another appeal."

"Great. So basically, we don't know exactly what to expect?"

"That's pretty much right. Just know that the audience will have some say in it. And they don't like boring."

"That should be easy. Martin and I are friends. The idea of kissing has never crossed our minds." Blakely looked a little guilty, like maybe she actually *had* been thinking about kissing her best friend. Probably a recent development. "We should be able to do boring and uninspired. Although, it'll be really hard to make it look like we've done it a million times before. And I care about him, so I might have to try to pretend that I don't."

"There's a difference between caring about someone as a friend and caring about someone to the point where you don't want to take your lips off his," Journee said, almost sounding wise if she did say so herself.

"You're my little sister. You're really not supposed to know more about this than I do."

"That's not my fault. Maybe you should have spent more of your teenaged years doing what everyone else was doing and a little less time immersed in your horses."

"I think it might be too late for me."

"You're really going to a lot of effort to try to avoid that football player. Is he that bad?"

Blakely crossed her arms over her chest and looked away. "He's probably not that bad. I just don't know. I don't want to know. I guess that shows that I'm shallow and pathetic."

"A little probably."

"Thanks."

"You want the truth. You're judging him based on what he does for a living. Or what he looks like. And that's wrong. You know that."

"I know."

"But don't be too hard on yourself. This is just an area where you don't do very well. And you have to do better. But there's no one that has a bigger heart than you do. You're always putting other people ahead of yourself. Look at the kids that you give lessons to without charging. And I did hear that a certain person was out at Martin's ranch, and you were showing your secret trick to her. Your competition. And you are helping her. That says a lot about your character. No one expects you to be perfect."

"She's my competition, true, but she's kind of a friend as well."

"She's not nearly as good a friend to you as you are to her. And you don't have to sugarcoat that. Because it's true. There aren't a lot of people who would have done what you did. Helped her, and she's giving you nothing in return. Nothing besides telling everyone how wonderful your best friend is and letting everyone know that she's got her eye on him." Journee didn't want Blakely to be too hard on herself. She had so many good qualities.

"Martin would never go for her."

Journee just raised her brows while Blakely very visibly tried not to squirm. It was so obvious someone would be snatching Martin up, especially if he were done on the rodeo circuit.

"You think Martin likes her?" she asked hesitantly.

Journee lifted a shoulder, striving for casual, so her sister didn't think she was hitting her over the head with anything. "You know better than I do."

Blakely sat for a bit and stared at her lap, thinking.

"Do you think I'm holding him back?" she asked softly.

"No. Martin isn't the kind of person who's gonna sit around and let someone walk all over him while he secretly pines away for something else. If he wants Erin, he'll go get her. You don't need to worry about that."

"Is there something you think I need to worry about?"

"I think you have to answer that question," Journee said enigmatically. "Now, there is something that I can do for you, since you're my older sister, and I love you."

"What's that?" Blakely asked, her eyes narrowing a bit in suspicion at Journee's tone.

Journee swallowed the laugh threatening to bubble up inside. "I can get that football player away from you. I think, most of the time, Mom and Dad are right, but if they're trying to match you up with him, they're definitely missing the mark on that one. I can make it so that you don't need to worry about him." She hadn't quite understood the question he'd asked when they'd met in front of the diner—she thought he'd said, did she work here? Which didn't make sense, since she'd just come from work in the ER and was still wearing her scrubs. She must have misheard him but hadn't had a chance to ask him to repeat himself. Not that it mattered.

"I wouldn't ask you to do that."

"I know. You didn't ask. I offered. You won't have to worry about running from him." Journee lifted a brow, indicating Blakely's position in the hayloft.

"I'm immature and stupid. We've already figured that out."

"No. You just don't have any experience in matters of the heart," Journee said, setting her notebook aside and rising, a small smile creeping out. "And that's not necessarily a bad thing. You don't have to know how to handle every man in the world. You just have to be faithful to one."

"You can't be faithful if you can't catch him."

"Maybe it's not a matter of catching, maybe it's a matter of being caught."

"He's not exactly been chasing me around."

"The football player?"

"He's obviously not a good match for me."

Journee nodded. "Usually, our parents have much better insight. I can hardly believe…" Absentmindedly, she fixed her shirt and brushed the hay off her pants, considering what her parents might be up to. She had her suspicions, but she couldn't voice them to her sister.

"Maybe they're just off their game."

"They can't be too far off. They just helped West and Poppy a few months ago."

"True." Blakely stood with Journee, following her to the loft ladder. "I guess they can't be right all the time. Just most of it."

Journee nodded. "They've definitely given me some good advice over the years. You'd be wise to listen to them. But I do agree with you on this. The ballplayer...he's not for you."

"Maybe he's for you."

Journee shook her head. "No." The little smile continued playing at the corners of her mouth. She was definitely more into Computer Geek. "But I think we could probably be friends."

She was two rungs down before she looked up at Blakely. "You stay here until I get him to take me to see the sheep with the triplets. I think they're two sheds down, and that should be far enough so that you can grab Martin and take the kids and do something."

"Thank you." Blakely said. "Just avoid the horse barn. And that's where I'll stay."

Chapter Ten

*D*ante's eyes widened in surprise as the woman he met coming out of the diner yesterday came down out of the hayloft. He couldn't recall her name, but he definitely remembered Blakely, the pastor's daughter he was supposed to be in the kissing contest with—but things had gone exactly the way Pastor Race had figured—who followed her a few steps behind.

He barely noticed Martin and Blakely embrace and didn't even think to be happy for them, because his eyes were caught on the dark-haired woman who came to him with a smile.

"I think we met yesterday," she said, her hand out.

"I think these were your kids yesterday, although today they seem to belong to someone else." He nodded his head at Frank and Darcy who were leaning on the top rung of the fence and watching what looked like maybe goats.

"My parents foster them. And I guess we all help out." She kind of leaned toward him and lowered her voice. "I kinda feel like God would like for me to adopt them. But I've been fighting it, because I think every child should have a mom and a dad. There's no dad in the picture here." Her voice held a little humor at the end, and he looked at her, blinking.

He'd never met a single woman who was interested in adopting. Not that there wasn't such a thing, he just didn't know any.

Mistletoe seemed like it was full of surprises.

"In case you've forgotten, my name's Journee." She held her hand out, and he grasped it, her hand feeling warm yet capable and somehow no-nonsense. It was the oddest sensation he'd ever gotten from shaking someone's hand.

Journee leaned toward him again, her eyes sparkling and a little smile playing around her lips. "Do you mind if we sneak out? I'd like to leave my sister and her friend alone. I think there's a romance budding there."

Lots of matchmakers in Mistletoe, too. Maybe he shouldn't stay. He already had someone he was interested in.

Journee grasped his arm, and he almost felt like a gentleman as they left the barn. Mistletoe was full of odd sensations. Considering his upbringing, he'd never felt like a gentleman before.

"I think the whole town is involved in the romance between Blakely and Martin. Your dad actually had me involved like five minutes after I met him for the first time."

Journee laughed. "That's my dad. I suppose he told you he used to be—"

"A heart surgeon. Yes. And now he works on—"

"Emotional hearts," she finished for him.

He'd never met anyone who, within five minutes, was finishing his sentences for him, and him hers.

It was odd the way he felt an instant connection to this woman.

Not even attraction, although there was that, but feeling like he knew her.

It was weird, and he honestly wondered again if she could be The Healing Pen. But she looked so confused when he asked if she worked in the ER.

Plenty of people wore scrubs. Dental assistants, nurses in doctors' offices, even any other nurse in the hospital.

He promised himself he wasn't going to think about it anymore, so he pushed it out of his head, thinking that The Healing Pen had promised to write while he was gone. If this were her, he should be hearing about it.

"Do you mind if we go to the sheep barn? There's an ewe with triplets, and I told Blakely that I would whisk you away."

"Are you whisking me away because you want Martin and her to get together? Or is it because Blakely hates football players?"

To her credit, she bit her lip and looked at him. "Someone told you that?"

"Yes, but from the way Blakely's been acting, I think I would have figured it out on my own regardless of what anyone said to me."

She giggled a little. "Blakely doesn't have a deceitful bone in her body. Whatever she's feeling is right there on her sleeve for everybody to see."

"And that's not you?" Somehow, that made him a little bit sad, to think that she might be smiling even if she were sad.

A shoulder lifted, and her fingers twitched in the crook of his arm. He liked that connection. Oddly.

"She's just big and wide and expressive. I guess I've always been more of a dreamer. I suppose I don't pretend to feel things that I don't, I just don't feel them as big as she does. Does that make sense?"

"That's something I can understand. On the team, there are guys who you never have to wonder what they're feeling, because whatever they're feeling is how they act and what they are. I don't think any of us would say we're in touch with our feelings. There are just people who have big celebrations in the end zone, and then there are the guys who dropped the ball and kinda smile a little. I suppose both are equally happy, just some of them express themselves in a bigger way."

"I can see that. Not that I've watched a lot of football, but I have brothers." She grinned a little, like that explained everything.

Not all men liked football, but he didn't correct her.

"So what kind of player are you?" Her question was casual, and she didn't seem to recognize him, but as small and unpretentious as this town was, and as into Christmas and farming and animals as they were, maybe football wasn't a big deal here.

"I suppose a mixture. I do a little more than smile when I make a touchdown. Especially if it's a big one."

"Like a game-winning touchdown?"

"Definitely."

"You score often?" she asked, turning the corner and indicating with her head the long white building ahead. They started toward it without any more direction.

"Forty-two in the last six years." Which was a record for the tight end position. "But who's counting, right?"

Her laugh rang out again. He found he wanted to do more to draw it out of her. "Sounds like someone is."

"It's kind of a big deal. I have the balls from my touchdowns. Well, some of the balls. I've given some of them away. I suppose eventually I'll give the other ones away as well."

"To family? I suppose your mother's pretty proud of you?"

"No. Kids who come and watch us practice. Training camp especially, they show up. The ones I gave away, I signed and gave away the next year at training camp."

"That's generous. They're worth money?"

"I guess. I've never looked them up, but probably."

"So your mother's living without a touchdown commemorating ball?"

"I haven't talked to her in a couple decades at least. I don't even know how I could get in touch with her, to be honest."

She stopped. Her head turned and tilted, and her eyes narrowed. "Really?"

He stopped beside her, but he didn't really look down at her. His eyes had been skimming over what he thought might be the obstacle course. At least, there were two chimneys set in what looked like the middle of the field, and some tables, and a few things that were covered with blankets. A small set of spectator stands sat off to the side.

"Yeah. Really. I guess I should feel lucky I wasn't aborted, because she didn't want me. She never really pretended she did. She and my dad spent most of my childhood fighting about who had to take me. I heard about other kids caught in custody battles, and while I felt bad for them, because nobody wants to see their parents fight, I was also slightly jealous. My parents never had a custody battle about who got me. But they had plenty of fights about who had to take me."

"Oh my goodness." Her tone held pity, and he hated that. He never told people about his past. Even in interviews, he glossed over it.

Somehow, he hadn't quite reached the point where he wished he hadn't said anything, but he definitely didn't want her pity. Not for this, and not from her.

"It made me a better person. Honestly. I learned to be scrappy and tough, and my childhood gave me grit. I can't regret it."

"I'll do that for you."

"Don't waste your time." The words came out a little shorter and more severe than he wanted. Especially to someone that he liked so well. He looked down in time to see a touch of hurt flash across her eyes, which didn't exactly surprise him.

"I'm sorry. I didn't mean to say it like that."

"It's fine. I'm just really blessed to have parents like Race and Penny. And I guess I was thinking about Darcy and Frank. Maybe the Lord has me talking to you for a reason."

"Raising a kid's a pretty big responsibility. It's brave of you to even think of doing it by yourself."

"Well, that's really where I'm stumbling. I don't want to. I'm hoping, and definitely praying, that God has a set of parents for them. But so far, no answers other than wait."

"That's the hardest one. I can take a no, and everyone loves a yes, but wait? That's tough."

"Agreed." They both stood, staring at the field with the chimneys in it.

"Your dad entered me in the obstacle contest. I'm guessing that's it." He nodded at the chimneys.

"You must be my partner. He needed one more couple. He asked me to do it and said he'd scrounge someone up for me."

"I guess he flipped over a few rocks and there I was."

"Oh boy. Maybe I just got the exact wrong impression, but I'm thinking you don't have any experience in participating in a Not Such an Ironman Ironman Contest?" Her voice seemed to hold a little hope, and he had to admit he started to feel a few butterflies fluttering in his stomach. This was just a small-town non-Christmas Christmas festival.

"No?"

Her lips flattened. "I'll see if I can get you a booklet of instructions, helpful hints, and secret tricks you can read before it starts tomorrow."

"Competition that stiff?"

"Typically, they have two high school kids, two young adults—which I'm guessing is us?—Two older ladies and two older gentlemen. The competition is fierce. Have you ever been beaten by your grandmother?"

"I didn't really have a grandmother." He almost wanted to eat the words as soon as they came out of his mouth, but they hung there in the air.

"I'm sorry," she said.

"Don't be."

He opened his mouth, but she spoke before he could.

"Is that the grit stuff you were talking about earlier? The stuff that makes you a good football player?"

"That's right."

"I'm sorry, please don't take this wrong, but I feel like family is more important than football."

"I wouldn't disagree with that. But you make the best out of what you get, and I feel like I've done that."

She nodded thoughtfully, looking at him.

She started to move, and her fingers slipped a little on his arm, but his hand came over and covered hers. Holding it there.

He wasn't exactly sure why he did that.

He was just...enjoying.

It was so uncanny the way she put him in mind of The Healing Pen.

It was a small town, there was no pressure to be the big football star, there wasn't even any pressure to keep his past hidden. He felt more comfortable with her than he had with anyone, ever, that he could remember, and yeah, he didn't want to lose the connection.

To cover the awkwardness of what he had obviously just done which was keep her from removing her hand from his arm, he said, "So are you serious about the handbook? Because I study our playbook all the time. There isn't a person on the team who knows it better than I do other than our QB, Rascal. And yeah, that's his name. The one his mom gave him. I feel like maybe his mom didn't like him too much when he was born, but maybe he grew on her, because she kept him. In contrast, Mom gave me an okay name, then she kinda ditched me, maybe when I lost my cuteness, I don't know."

He had been trying to make a joke, but he should have known that he couldn't really joke about something like that with people who didn't know him. He and Rascal joked about it all the time.

Actually, she took it better than he was afraid she was going to. A shadow crossed her face, and her lips turned down a little, but then she smiled.

"Running joke?"

He nodded. "Can't change it. There's no point in getting upset about it. It is what it is. I used it to my advantage. I'm not gonna cry about it for the rest of my life."

She nodded. "I like that."

Chapter Eleven

ante felt like a kid in kindergarten who had just had his teacher praise him. It was a good feeling. But also scared him a little that this woman whom he'd just met, barely knew, could make him feel like he'd done something praiseworthy. When he really hadn't done anything at all.

He kind of forgot it was his turn to talk while her eyes, green and filled with humor and somehow mesmerizing, locked with his.

There were a thousand things that ran through his head, things he wanted to say, ask her, and probably the top question of all was one that was impossible.

After meeting Race and talking to him, he had even more respect for the man and didn't want to break the conditions of being a pen pal.

"I was kidding," she finally said.

He'd been out with a lot of girls. He hadn't been kidding when he'd said that to The Healing Pen, but honestly, the time he'd spent with those girls had been more about him than them. He wasn't sure how to tell if a girl was seriously interested in him, for him, and not for the prestige of having him.

Something told him Journee was that kind of girl. The kind of girl like The Healing Pen. The kind who didn't really care about prestige and was more interested in him for himself.

Maybe that was why it was so easy for things he never told anyone to fall off his tongue.

Her words finally penetrated his brain, and he said, "Kidding about what?"

She shook her head. "There's no playbook for the Not Such an Ironman Ironman Contest." She closed one eye though and gritted her teeth a little. "But it *is* pretty competitive. Maybe having your grandmother beat you isn't too bad, but having the elementary school kids win? It's embarrassing."

"Sounds like you had experience in this?"

"I have. I did it with my brother Shawn one year, and he ate the gingerbread instead of making a gingerbread house out of it. And if that wasn't bad enough, he got stuck in the chimney. Not because he couldn't fit, but because he put one leg out the top and one leg down and ended up doing kind of a split..." She shook her head. "Don't ask me why. It was Shawn. He's weird. Anyway. I have trouble with claustrophobia, and I still managed to get up and down it. Still. We lost. Like last place." She cleared her throat. "And in case you forgot what it's like to be an elementary school kid, they tease you. Big time. And lord it over you. And taunt. And they pay their friends to throw rotten fruit." She shivered. "If that's not bad enough, the losers of the Not Such an Ironman Ironman Contest are the first people on the block for the pie-throwing contest. Not to throw the pie," she added hastily. "But to have the pie thrown at you."

"Let me guess. The first people to get to throw pies are the kids who beat you."

"Bingo."

"Wow. Small towns have a sadistic streak."

"Exactly. We look innocuous, but it's a ruse. We are absolutely cutthroat about our festivals." This time, both eyes narrowed. "Think Super Bowl, on steroids."

"Now the woman's talking my language." He grinned a little. "I don't have a ring, but I intend to get one."

"There's no ring here. Just the freedom from cream pies. And I'm talking actual cream pies. That's not some kind of slang term for cow patties. I promise. Or, honestly, I would be insisting that we practice."

"Wow. Me too. Definitely, if we were talking cow patties, I would insist on practicing. In case you haven't noticed, I'm really not a country boy."

"I noticed. Trust me. Everyone here has noticed."

"What? Is it stamped on my forehead?"

"I think it's the loafers. Not that country boys can't wear loafers, it's just most of them usually wear boots. Or maybe it's the way you walk, or…I don't know. But yeah. Actually, it's probably because everybody knows everybody, and no one knows you."

"I think your sister said something about me having more muscles than brains. I'm assuming that wasn't a compliment?"

Journee grimaced. "I'm sorry. No. Not a compliment." She bit her lip and looked him over. The look made his skin warm in a not uncomfortable way. "The muscles do kind of make you stick out. Sorry."

Dante stared at her, nodding a little and unsure of what to say. This was the first time in his life that he had any hint or clue that a woman might not be totally into his muscles.

Still, her look had done crazy things to his insides.

He'd been teased about being a dumb jock before, plenty of times. But he'd always assumed that his physique was, at least, appealing.

The idea that it wasn't, that it was actually something that made him stand out, and in an implied bad way, was new.

He kind of wanted to blame it on the small town, but he had a feeling that wasn't entirely accurate.

Still, she seemed to respect what he did, just not in a hero worship kind of way.

It was a change that he thought he might like.

"If you don't mind, I probably ought to get back to my mom. I took a little bit of time off for a lunch break. That's what I was doing when Blakely found me in the hayloft."

"Of course not. This festival seems like it's a pretty big deal for your small town," he said as she put a little pressure on his arm, and he turned with her toward a back alley which led to the main street of town.

"It is. People have started to depend on the Christmas tourism to make enough money to stay solvent throughout the year. It's a curse and a blessing."

"I think I see that. Extra money means extra people, and sometimes, extra people means all the problems that come with people."

"Exactly."

"Well, I'm free for the rest of the day. Maybe your mom can put me to work too."

"You might regret saying that, because I can guarantee you she will." Journee smiled up at him, and he looked down, wonder swelling his heart.

How could he be happy like this, in a small town, with a simple girl beside him, heading off to help with a festival?

A rhetorical question, he supposed. Because it just demonstrated all the changes that had been happening in him since the accident. It was hard to deny that the Lord was most definitely working in his life.

Still, there was a tug of unease. While he was pretty sure his feelings for Journee were friend only, and he had no idea if there would ever be anything between The Healing Pen and him, he couldn't help but feel somewhat disappointed.

He felt a tug for both women; he had thought he'd left the multiple dating scene behind.

Maybe he was too engrossed in his thoughts, or maybe it would have happened anyway, but they'd barely taken three steps when a dog, his leash dragging, followed not so closely by a boy screaming, "Rusty! Come back here, Rusty!" charged directly toward them.

Everything would have been just fine, since the dog ran by with no problems, but the leash got tangled up in Journee's legs, and she stumbled, bumping into him, which caused him to step into the boy's path, and somehow, his foot got caught in the leash, or maybe it was the dog yanking Journee that hit his foot at the same time, but whatever it was, the dog, the boy, Journee, and he all ended up on the ground together.

Journee and the boy were both immediately working on getting the dog's leash untangled, but he didn't move for a few moments, because Journee's shoulder bag had come loose, and the notebook inside had fallen out, landing right beside his head, open.

He didn't need to see the salutation—Dear Computer Geek—to recognize the handwriting that he'd looked forward to receiving for the last five months.

Journee was The Healing Pen.

Chapter Twelve

Dear Computer Geek,

I guess we never talked about where you live, but I always assumed you were not from a small town.

So let me explain a small-town festival to you.

It's crazy.

That's pretty much all you need to know.

Expect to see things you've never seen before.

I'm not talking about like wonders of the world. There's nothing like an Egyptian pyramid in in my town.

Of course not.

But I suppose every town has things that make it unique, and they capitalize on those things.

My town has Christmas.

And so Christmas in July capitalizes on everything that makes us different from every other town in America.

That, and we have some pretty crazy people here too.

Take the pie-throwing contest.

We take the losers from all of the contests that they have, and I know it's not politically correct to say losers, but we do here. Anyway, we take the losers, and we throw pies at them.

Like I said, not politically correct. But definitely unique.

Because I know this is going to be a question, I'm going to answer it right now: yes, I have most definitely been the object of our pie-throwing contest.

I bet you have no idea how hard it is to get whipped cream out of your ear.

And no, I have no idea how, when someone throws a pie at your face, you get whipped cream in your ear.

Just trust me on this. It happens.

I hope your trip is going well.

Enjoying the festival,

The Healing Pen

"You and Dante seemed to be having a good time yesterday." Burgundy, Journee's friend who'd recently married and was settled happily outside of Mistletoe, studied her fingernails as she spoke casually. She looked up with a little grin and a twinkle in her eye. "In fact, you seem to be having a *very* good time."

Journee smiled a little. She wasn't afraid to admit it. "He was nice. And funny."

"You say that like you're surprised."

"I guess I have a stereotype in my head of football players. I suppose because of Blakely or maybe just because of living in cattle country and growing up watching rodeos."

"Wow. So judgmental."

"I know. But people say unkind things about others just because they live in a small town. You know it."

Burgundy nodded, grinning. "I keep giving you a hard time, but I know exactly what you're saying. People can deny it all they want to, but we all have things we kind of think, just because of our experiences. I think maybe even a hundred years ago, that was considered normal, and now we're made to feel guilty about it."

"Well, we should, at least a bit, since a lot of times the things we think are negative."

"I know. I've actually experienced those to some extent."

Burgundy's voice kind of trailed off at the end, and Journee put an arm around her, squeezing her, as they walked down Main Street, looking at the different vendors and listening to the Christmas music that was piped out of strategically placed speakers.

Strategically placed, because the entire town could hear the music.

"I'm sorry."

Burgundy shrugged. "Don't be. A lot of times, stereotypes are stereotypes because they're true. They help us relate to the world around us. I suppose there's a lot more psychology involved, but I wouldn't knock yourself out too hard about it, because everybody does it."

"Well, regardless, I think the one about Dante was completely untrue. He turned out to be a really nice guy, and yeah, it surprised me. But yeah. I had a good time with him."

Journee thought for a minute or two about the letters she'd written to Computer Geek.

She hadn't mentioned what she'd done at the festival, exactly. She'd just given an overview.

And she hadn't talked about Dante at all. She wasn't sure why.

She wasn't sure she wanted to examine her motives too closely, because she didn't really feel either man was a romantic prospect, exactly. But especially not Dante.

Still, she supposed the fact that she didn't give specifics in her letter probably said something that she wasn't ready to think about.

"Are you seeing him again today? You guys meeting somewhere?" Burgundy bumped Journee's shoulder with hers, then wiggled her eyebrows.

"You're a good one to talk. Where's Crew?" Journee asked, referring to Burgundy's new husband.

"He promised Mrs. Scholz he'd be in the dancing contest with her."

Journee stopped short, her mouth half open. Neither Mrs. Scholz nor Crew seemed like the dancing kind of people.

Finally, she managed to get one word out. "Oh?"

"I know. It's nuts." Burgundy giggled. "You should see them at home."

Journee tried to picture Crew, who always seemed kind of taciturn and slightly intimidating, and Mrs. Scholz, who was a crusty old lady and did not seem like a dancer.

"The odd couple. That would almost make the dancing contest worth watching."

"Definitely. Especially if they play 'Rockin' Around the Christmas Tree' for them, which I specifically requested. It's Mrs. Scholz's favorite song, and I know Crew is my husband, but he is absolutely adorable when he's dancing with Mrs. Scholz." Burgundy's voice lowered a little, and her love for her husband was absolutely clear in her words.

Journee smiled, an odd feeling pinching her throat. Not jealousy. She was happy for her friend, but she'd love to be able to talk about somebody like that. With a lot of dreamy sweetness in her voice.

But she wasn't sure she wanted to risk so much again. There was a lot of pain involved when it didn't work out.

"When does it start?" Journee figured she'd enjoy watching it, but she didn't want to be late for the Not Such an Ironman Ironman Competition.

"We have about thirty minutes. I figured if I moseyed on down there, I'd get there in time to see the beginning. If Mrs. Scholz doesn't win, she's gonna want me to give her a critique of all of the other contestants, since she'll be waiting in the back." Burgundy crossed her arms over her chest and stopped in the middle of the sidewalk, eyeing Journee. "Now, you didn't answer my question."

Journee laughed. "I forgot your question. The idea of Crew and Mrs. Scholz dancing together pretty much threw everything else out of my head."

"Dante? Hello? You guys look good together. And happy."

"We're happy. We're friends. But that's it. Friends. Nothing more."

"Hmm. Okay. My question was are you going to see him again?"

"We're in the Not Such an Ironman Ironman Contest together. I think Dad signed us up." Journee said that last sentence casually, and she wasn't quite sure why she added it.

Burgundy was already doing a lot of hinting around, and her dad kind of had a reputation in town for being a bit of a matchmaker.

Burgundy didn't say anything, just pressed her lips together and had a look on her face that kind of said "I told you so."

Journee was about to ask her if she wanted company watching the dancing contest, at least for the beginning part of it, but Dante came out of the diner just ahead of them, and when he looked up the street and saw them, his face lit up with a smile and he started toward them.

"That's a look of a guy who's happy to see someone," Burgundy said out of the corner of her mouth.

"So you guys have met?" Journee said, just a little tongue-in-cheek. She didn't think that Dante was any more into her than she was into him.

And she wasn't into him.

She thought that might be a little bit of a lie, but she wasn't so far gone that she couldn't come back.

She was fairly certain of that anyway. Even as she felt her own face light up and break into a smile that matched his.

She'd had a good time with him yesterday.

"Good morning, ladies," Dante said as he reached them, stopping and shoving a hand in his pocket, filling his T-shirt quite nicely, the way she would expect a football player to do.

It didn't hurt anything for her to admire that.

"Morning, Dante. This is Burgundy. She's on her way to the dancing contest to watch her husband dance with another woman."

Burgundy laughed out loud at that, and she held up her phone. "I'm even going to videotape it." She held her hand out to Dante, who took it and shook. "Good to meet you, Dante, I'm going to head out and see if I can get a good seat for the contest. Mrs. Scholz will have my hide if I don't get a video of the entire thing."

They murmured some goodbyes before Burgundy hurried off.

"I take it Mrs. Scholz must be an older lady?"

Journee nodded. "I've never heard an exact age, but I would say upwards of eighty. She and Crew will definitely make an interesting couple."

"Maybe we could try to see them, although we're supposed to be at the Not Such an Ironman Ironman Contest early so we can go over the rules. Apparently, they're slightly different than they were last year. I just got done talking to Pastor Race."

"I think they change every year. Thanks for the heads-up though."

"Hey, we need all the help we can get if we're not going to end up in the pie-throwing contest. As the targets." He grinned. "Can't say I wouldn't mind throwing pies at a few people. None of them are probably here today."

"Oh really? Teammates?"

He just grinned.

She shook her head.

They had turned and started walking slowly in the general direction of the Ironman contest, which would take them behind the crowd of people watching the dancing contest. Honestly, after talking to Burgundy, Journee was a little disappointed she wasn't going to get to see it.

But Dante was right; she didn't want to lose the Not Such an Ironman Ironman Contest. She didn't mind coming in any place but last, as she didn't want to end up in the pie-throwing contest.

"It might be a good idea to get there a little early so we can size up our competition. We just have to beat one of them."

"Great minds think alike. Although, I have to admit, any time I enter a competition, my mind is always on winning. This is the first time I'm like 'I just don't want to lose.'"

They laughed. "Maybe that would be a little more inspiring for pro ball, if there were cream pies involved."

"I don't know. I could almost see the guys not caring as long as they got to eat whatever was thrown at them. How tasty are the pies anyway?"

"No. We are not even going to go there. You are not giving up. We are not going to end up with pies on our faces."

"There should be some kind of inspiration to try to win. What's the award? I've never even heard. All I hear about are the pies," he said as they turned down the alley, nodding to a couple other people who were coming out.

"That's a good question. I have no idea. Maybe you get to stand on the platform and they play the American anthem or something."

"That's the Olympics, not Ironman competitions."

"Okay. I'll take your word for it. I've never actually watched an Ironman competition."

The crowd for the dancing competition cheered as Mrs. Densmore, the MC for the event, announced the competitors and stated the rules.

Dante leaned down. "Too bad we couldn't have entered this one.

I think I'm much better at dancing than I am at going down chimneys."

She stretched up, still not tall enough to reach his ear. He had to bend over.

"So you've gone down a chimney before?" She allowed there to be a lot of hope in her voice.

He gave a cheesy smile. "No?"

"Man, that was going to be such an asset. I was really feeling hopeful."

"I could tell. The pie thing really scares you, doesn't it?"

"It does. It's embarrassing, not to mention it hurts if the edge of the pie plate hits you in the face. You know, what you see on TV where somebody throws a pie and it hits them perfectly in the face with the top of the pie. That's great. But what about people who don't throw very well? The pies that hit you with the rim of the pie plate. I'm telling you, it hurts. And you're not allowed to lift your hand up and keep it from hitting. Not only that but something else that people never think about is whenever you get hit in the face with a pie, you can't breathe."

"You're right. I never thought about that."

"Maybe this makes me weird, but I kind of like to breathe. It bothers me when I can't."

"No. I think that's pretty normal. I feel the same way anyway."

"So, yeah, of course it's embarrassing to get a pie in the face in front of people, but there are other factors to take into consideration."

"Well, shouldn't we lose just to save anyone else from going through that kind of suffering?"

She stopped, her jaw dropping, and she stared him. "You're kidding, right?"

"No. Someone has to do it. It might as well be us."

"I think I'm going to see if I can get a different partner."

"Maybe that's my strategy. If I get fired as your partner, I definitely won't get a pie thrown at me, right?"

"If you get fired as my partner…I have a little bit of clout in this town, and I will make sure that you are on that stage getting a pie thrown at you. Somehow."

"Clout? You have clout?"

"I do. I happen to be related to the organizer of the festival. And I think I can approach it from the angle of you're some kind of big-name football player. People should recognize you and enjoy the chance to throw a pie at you. Especially the visitors to the town." She let her eyes sweep over the crowded field in front of the stage where the dancing contest was to take place. "Surely some of these people know you. And since we have speakers that can reach the entire town, it will be a simple matter of announcing that anyone who wants to throw pie at the big-name football player can do so. Actually, I think there are people who would pay for the privilege. This could be a big moneymaker."

"I feel like I'm being blackmailed."

"For a big guy, you're pretty in touch with your feelings." Both of them had been walking with smiles on their faces, and kind of by mutual agreement, they'd stopped in the middle of the back of the crowd of people, just keeping an eye on the stage as Mrs. Densmore finished up the rules and the introductions.

"I think we have time to watch one of these, if you want to." His brows lifted, as though it were all up to her.

"I don't know where Crew and Mrs. Scholz are in the program, but I hope they're first. Because I'd really like to see them."

As they spoke, Mrs. Densmore announced the first competitors. Journee and he exchanged glances as she called out Crew and Mrs. Scholz's names.

"Looks like we get to have everything," Dante said low.

"I'll agree with you after we don't lose the Not Such an Ironman Ironman contest. And not one second before."

"Wow. She drives a hard bargain." He didn't say any more as the strains of "Rockin' Around the Christmas Tree" came over the speakers.

Crew, dressed in a Santa outfit, shuffled on the stage with Mrs. Scholz. Her orthopedic shoes clumped right next to the boots he wore, and her movements were endearingly jerky, while Crew seemed to be too nervous to relax and enjoy his performance.

"This is one of those things you just can't take your eyes away for a second," Dante said, leaning down but, as he said, not taking his eyes away for a second. "Because I'm almost positive that Mrs. Scholz is going to poke one of his eyes out, and while I don't really want to see that, I can't stop watching."

"I feel the exact same way," Journee said, containing a giggle but just barely, her eyes never leaving the stage either because he was right. It was just so obvious that one of her seemingly random finger pokes in the air was going to connect with Crew's eye socket that it was impossible to look away or even blink.

Not to mention the rest of their movements were hilarious in an adorable, they-are-so-cute-together kind of way.

"They definitely know how to tear up the boards," Dante said, shaking his head and chuckling softly.

"And entertain. I don't think there's a single person here who hasn't belly laughed almost the entire way through this." It was true, the entire crowd of people were just laughing and roaring to the point they could barely hear the music, which was really loud.

Finally, as the song drew to a close, Mrs. Scholz leaned backward ever so slightly, lifted one leg from the ground, her orthopedic shoe dangling in the air, her knee bent, her fingers still pointed out in all directions while Crew had his arm behind her back, facing the audience, one big leg bent, and the other stretched out in front of him, his boot heel on the floor.

The song ended, and the entire audience erupted in cheers and clapping, most of them still laughing, as Journee and Dante were.

"That has to be one of the funniest things I've ever seen," Dante said, several minutes later as the noise started to dissipate enough that they could be heard.

"I've got a feeling there's going to be a new dance craze sweeping the nation."

"Yeah, the poke your eye out bunny clop." Dante checked his watch. "We'd better get going. We don't want to miss a second of the instructions, giving ourselves every advantage we possibly can since someone is petrified of losing."

"You can't tell me that you want to lose."

"I'm not afraid to lose. Actually, the odds are the same here as for a ball game, you're either gonna win or you're gonna lose."

She nodded slowly.

"I'm not used to losing." He opened his mouth like he wanted to say more, and then he snapped it shut. A father, holding a child in his arms and holding onto the hand of another, walked toward them, leaning down to hear what his son was saying.

Dante grabbed Journee's hand and pulled her out of the man's path.

The man, realizing that he'd almost run into someone, looked up. "I'm sorry. Excuse me."

"It's okay."

"Don't worry about it."

They spoke together, probably looking goofy because after laughing their way through Crew and Mrs. Schultz's dance routine, everything seemed funny.

"Thanks. I was still thinking about the dancing competition. There is absolutely no way anyone could beat that. They're definitely the winners, now all anyone else would be dancing for would be to not have the pie thrown in their face."

"I have to agree with that. I can only hope that we do the Not Such an Ironman Ironman competition that well."

"Me too."

His hand was large, and he didn't let go as they started walking again.

She wasn't sure why, but she didn't pull her hand away.

Chapter Thirteen

Dante had held plenty of girls' hands. It shouldn't have been that big of a deal to him.

He couldn't help but notice the look on her face as he took it and then held it and didn't let go.

Just fleeting expressions. It wasn't like she made a big deal about it. But the surprise, and a bit of wonder, and something else, something that made him feel like it wasn't something that she did every day and it was special to her.

He liked that idea. The idea that what was between them could be special.

He hoped it could be more. Wanted more, now that he knew she was The Healing Pen.

Funny, since he'd only technically known her for a few days, but she felt so familiar because he knew her through her letters.

Time had flown by a little faster than what they thought maybe, because when they got to the area where the Not Such an Ironman Ironman Contest was to take place, it looked like everyone else was there. At least, there was a whole group of people, and a man with a clipboard and a big bushy beard stood in front of them.

He looked up as they approached. "Journee. I was starting to think I was going to have to call you over the loudspeaker. That must be Dante with you."

"I'm sorry. We stopped to watch the dancing competition, it was really good," Journee said with a grin, which the man returned.

He didn't seem upset, although he did look at his watch. They were starting the instructions a few minutes early anyway.

"I'm George Albright, and I'm in charge of supervising this competition. The judges are gathering over there." The man nodded to a table where several older ladies and a couple of middle-aged ones were chatting and arranging chairs at a rectangular table.

Dante listened with half an ear as the man gave the instructions for the contest. His focus was more on the woman beside him. He hadn't expected to like her so much so fast. He'd been interested in The Healing Pen, sure. Interested in a curious and mostly superficial way.

Maybe it was something with small-town girls. Since he hadn't been around many.

He could admit there could be more than friend feelings between them. But he wouldn't let anything happen. Not yet. It hadn't been his fault that her notebook had opened where he could see it. But he didn't want Race to think he was doing something he'd promised not to.

He still had over six months to wait.

That didn't mean he couldn't enjoy today. Couldn't start hoping she would come to like him as much as he liked her.

He glanced over the course as George Albright talked about putting a gingerbread house together, upside down.

A smile tugged out Dante's lips as he looked over at Journee, who was grinning at him.

"Not your skill set?" she whispered, one brow cocked at a goofy angle.

He shook his head. "Even a right-side-up house would be a struggle."

Her eyes twinkled, and maybe their gazes held just a second longer than necessary. The oddest sensation tripped through his chest, and he had to clamp his teeth over the words that wanted to come out.

"And both of the members of your team have to go down the chimney and back up. If you are over fifty years old, you can have one of your grandchildren do that for you; however, they may not start until you are there, and they have to follow all the same rules that you do."

"Really? You hit fifty, and you don't have to do the chimney thing?" He leaned over to Journee, who grinned up at him.

"It is called the Not Such an Ironman Ironman Contest for a reason. I suppose it's living up to its name right there. But it hardly seems fair, doesn't it?" She bit her lip in mock consternation. "Do you think we should complain?"

"I've a feeling if we did, they'd totally let us out of it. But who would we get to take our places?"

"Forget that. The whole point is to have fun, and while I'm claustrophobic, part of the fun is stepping out of your comfort zone." Her lips pursed. "I really don't want to. But still, that's kind of beside the point."

"I think that is the point," he said with a smirk.

They laughed softly together, garnering a few looks from the people sitting next to them. But he didn't really care.

He was having more fun with this than he expected. Probably because of his partner. He supposed this was the kind of thing that in normal times he would have tried to get out of. But he had definitely been looking forward to spending the day with Journee, spending his time with her, and he was almost certain that was new for him, because beyond football and working on coding, he didn't do too many other things solely for fun.

He hadn't been interested.

But maybe he just hadn't had the right partner.

"All right, and new this year is making a Christmas tree out of decorations." Mr. Albright paused a little there to let the idea sink in. Dante had heard that in a typical contest, contestants were to decorate a Christmas tree. Now apparently instead of decorating a tree, they were making a tree.

"I'm a little skeptical on this one, because everybody's going to have different decorations. Mr. Wynn and his wife enjoy going to estate sales, and sometimes, they come back with boxes of decorations." Mr. Albright paused again. "It's a long story, but just trust me, Mr. Wynn was more than happy to get some of these things out of his attic." There were some titters going through the crowd.

Journee leaned over to him, and he bowed his head down. "Mrs. Wynn is something of a packrat. They probably have enough decorations in their attic, their basement, and their garage to supply one hundred competitions like this."

He nodded, thinking that it was sweet that at least Mr. Wynn and Mrs. Wynn had enough in common that they enjoyed going to those sales together. If something that they did together resulted in an excess, at least they were doing something smart with it.

They listened a little more as the stands around them filled and a crowd formed along the yellow tape line.

By the time Mr. Albright was done and said the competition would start in ten minutes, Dante couldn't believe how many people had gathered.

"I don't think this is going to be too hard," Dante said as he looked around at their competitors. "At least, I don't think we'll come in last." He lifted his brows and looked at Journee, wanting her to confirm his optimistic statement.

"Well, when he told us that we had to go cut down our own Christmas tree and the woods is down there," she nodded her head at a copse of trees a mile away, "I kinda figured that unless we really mess something else up, we're going to be good. Because I don't think there's another set of competitors who can beat us down and back. Of course, getting it done fast isn't the only thing that matters, but it is one thing." Her voice ended on a hopeful note, and he nodded to encourage her.

"We're definitely the favorites for that one." He looked over at the elderly couple beside them. And then at the two kids who looked like they were maybe twelve. Even the middle-aged couple probably wouldn't be able to beat them to that.

"If our goal is to simply keep from getting pies thrown at us, I think we're good." He tried to infuse confidence in his voice, because there was just a nagging feeling about this competition, something he couldn't quite define, that made him think that maybe they weren't going to do as well as what he was hoping. He tried to shove that feeling aside.

In his experience, when he played a game, how he thought he was going to do was often how he did. He needed to think that they were going to win. And shove the doubt aside.

"Any strategies or tips I should be aware of?" he asked.

"They changed everything around this year. Which they often do. It's never been the same two years in a row. I think that's part of what keeps it so popular. But the whole cutting the Christmas tree down and the upside-down gingerbread house...I have no idea how to do that. How are we going to get it to stand up?"

"Why can't we make a gingerbread house right side up and then just turn it upside down when we're finished?" That seemed logical to him.

"That makes sense," she said, the tone of her voice implying that she should have thought about that herself. "I mean, that makes a lot more sense than building it upside down to begin with. But how can we get it to stand up?"

He thought for a second. Design wasn't necessarily his thing, at least not physical design. "Chimneys?"

She started nodding immediately. "Great thought. I think we can do that. Pretty easily."

Even while he agreed with her, he was still almost overcome with that odd feeling that something was going to go wrong.

"Okay, everyone. You see the stations where you make the gingerbread house and the Christmas tree. Obviously, you can see the chimneys. That table is where you get your gift-wrapping assignment. And right there on that far table are the hand saws to go cut yourselves down a Christmas tree. Anything that wasn't gone over in the rules is fair game." Mr. Albright winked. At least, it looked like a wink.

Dante's nose wrinkled, and he looked down at Journee, wondering if she had seen the same thing he did.

She turned her head and met his gaze, the same questions in her eyes that he felt in his, but she shrugged. Almost like she was saying she had no clue what was going on with that.

Then as her eyes moved back forward, she got a big smile on her face and waved.

Dante followed her gaze and saw, standing over on the edge, Blakely and her friend Martin. He nodded at Martin, who grinned back at him, almost laughing like he knew that the whole point of this was not to win but to avoid the pies.

He also felt like Martin maybe understood the whole reason he was standing here.

It wasn't because he wanted to participate in the festival, and he wasn't even sure how much of it was because Race had asked him to.

His eyes caught on the dark head beside him. He was pretty sure the whole reason he was here was right there.

Weird. He couldn't recall ever doing anything this crazy before, and definitely not for a girl.

Although, he knew plenty of guys who had done really crazy things for their women.

He'd never thought he would join those ranks.

His leg gave him a little twitch as they moseyed to the starting line. It was the first time today that he'd felt it, despite having taken a three-mile run when he woke up this morning.

He made a mental note to make sure he was doing the exercises his trainer had given him down to the letter. Training camp was just a week away, and he didn't want to show up out of shape.

He was confident he wasn't, spending several hours in the gym each evening.

Regardless, he definitely felt he was in good enough shape to be able to run down and get a Christmas tree and, seriously, at least not come in last in this small-town festival contest.

How hard could it be?

Chapter Fourteen

This was going to be easy.

The upside-down gingerbread house had thrown her for a bit, but Dante had come up with a really great solution.

Obviously, as a pro ballplayer, there was a whole block of his life that she really knew nothing about, but she was pretty sure that he would almost have to have a competitive streak the proverbial mile wide.

He wouldn't want to lose.

She didn't either, but more because of the pie.

Regardless, she figured he was probably aiming slightly higher, and she would do her best to accommodate.

There were five stations, and everyone was starting out at a different station, even though there was room at each station for more than one team to participate.

As Mr. Albright drew names and assigned each couple to a station, Dante shifted beside her from foot to foot.

She assumed that meant he was nervous.

She had to admit, as Mr. Albright pulled their names and assigned them to the chimney first, her own stomach was flipping.

She didn't think she could blame it all on the pies.

"Nervous?" Dante leaned over and asked as they walked to the line in front of the chimneys.

She nodded. "Is that terrible? I mean, it's just a small-town festival."

"I don't think so. Just my opinion, but I've played in some pretty big ball games, in front of a lot of people, and this is definitely right up there in the nervousness department. In fact, I'm not sure I've ever been quite this worked up."

She eyeballed him. The very most he was doing was shifting from one foot to another, and that only occasionally.

"You don't really look nervous."

His grin was self-effacing. "Normally, before a ball game, I don't talk. At all. Just totally focus on my role in the game, the game plan, the opposing team, and what the coaches have said. You know, getting my head right. For some reason, I'm talking. I think that pretty much shows the extent of my nervousness."

"I guess if you say so. I just know I feel like I'm going to throw up, and that's telling me I'm nervous. Or that I have the stomach flu. It's pretty much the same thing, isn't it?"

He laughed. "Let's not talk about the flu."

"Yeah, that would be pretty bad. He didn't say anything about stopping the time to have bathroom breaks."

"If you desert me, I can't guarantee that I'm going to stand up on that stage and become a pie target by myself."

"I don't think I can desert you. I have to live here. If you skip out, you never have to show your face in town again."

He looked at her, almost like he was going to say something, like he was going to deny that. But she was right. He didn't have to come back to town.

He was a big-name ballplayer, in town because of the friendship between his coach and her dad. She could almost guarantee he wouldn't be back.

And maybe, when he left, she'd have lost a friend, but nothing more.

"Everyone, get ready. I'm gonna start the timer in five, four, three…"

Journee took a deep breath and threw a tremulous smile in Dante's direction. His face looked stern, serious, and focused.

It looked the opposite of everything she felt.

"… Two, one…begin!"

There was no gunshot; they didn't even ring a cow bell. But Christmas music did immediately start blasting out of the speakers.

Journee found it a little distracting as they hurried over the chimney.

"He said we had to go up and down, so that's kind of the opposite of what you'd expect Santa to do but shouldn't be too hard." Dante bent over and looked in the makeshift fireplace. "How sturdy do you think this thing is?" he asked as he wiggled the stones.

"It's probably a good question for you, since you're the biggest guy here. If it's not going to last through someone climbing it, you're probably the one."

Dante froze, then turned slowly to look at her. "I think she just called me fat."

"I think he's digging for compliments on his muscular physique. How about we focus on the competition, and we can talk about your muscles later?"

"Now she just called me a dumb jock."

She laughed. "This is a great time for you to get supersensitive."

"Hey, big guys have feelings too."

"I thought guys didn't have feelings?" she asked, bending over beside him and looking up the chimney. "Do you want me to go first?"

"I think chivalry demands it," he said, kinda sounding sarcastic.

"When you hold open doors, you let the ladies walk through first. When it comes to going up chimneys, it's men first every time."

"Man, I knew I should have brought my etiquette book along."

She couldn't even think of the retort for that, because he just looked so hilarious standing there, the tough football player, almost twice as big as she was, making a smart comment about his etiquette book.

"I'll let you borrow mine. Not now. Both of us need to conquer this chimney."

"Exactly. And we're wasting time debating about it." He paused, eyeing her up. "Rock paper scissors?"

She jerked her head down. "Done."

They both held their fists out. "Rock, paper, scissors, shoot!"

Her rock beat his scissors.

He smirked. "Guess that means you go first."

"Wait. I won."

"I know. That means you go first."

Half amused, half exasperated, she hunched over again. She really was going to have to go up the chimney first. She didn't want to.

"Have I ever mentioned my issues with claustrophobia?"

"I totally understand. I have the same fear of horses."

This wasn't the time for her to get the giggles, but she had to laugh over that. "What does that have to do with anything? We're looking at the chimney. There're no horses in sight."

"I just wanted you to know I commiserate with you."

"You know, I feel like I need to petition the Board of Directors to have a horse race in the Ironman contest next year."

"I think I am going to be busy next July. Maybe training camp will start early."

"Nice." She peered up the chimney, knowing that it made sense for her to go up first.

The conversation had been quick, and most people were still moseying over to their places. The contest wasn't all about getting the best timing, although finishing quickly did count.

"All right, I'm just gonna close my eyes and do this."

She bent over and took a breath. She wasn't joking about being claustrophobic.

He put his hand on her arm and said softly, "Hey. I'll go first. I was just teasing you."

"No, I was going along with the joking, but it just makes sense for me to do it first since I'm smaller, and honestly, that's not meant as an insult. If it's not that sturdy, we'll find out now. Although, I really am claustrophobic. I was in a foster home for a little while growing up, and that was one of the punishments. Being locked in a closet."

"Oh. That sounds awful." He truly sounded like he meant it.

She hadn't meant to say anything and didn't want to make a big deal out of it. She tried to downplay it. "It was at the time. I'm over it now. But I had five siblings, and I was used to doing everything with them, and that was probably half of the problem, that I was alone in that closet. Not just that it was dark and I couldn't get out."

She shivered. Looking back, she could be rational that nothing was going to happen to her in the dark closet, but at the time, she'd been petrified. Rightfully so, just being a young child who had recently lost her parents.

"Wow, I feel kinda bad even mentioning the horse thing. I just fell off one, you know, like every other kid in the world. Although I happened to break my arm. I haven't ridden one since. And yeah, I can see the wisdom behind the whole adage about falling off a horse and getting right back on, because so many years have gone by and I avoid the whole idea of even being around horses. Because there's this thought in the back of my head that it hurts." He looked around, although they were the only ones at the chimneys. "Don't tell anyone. Kinda ruins my tough-guy image."

She was hunched down in the fireplace, trying to get up enough nerve to stand up. That was probably the first step in getting up the chimney. "Trust me. Your secret is safe with me."

She meant that as a joke, or maybe flippantly, but rather than smile, he kind of grimaced, and she got the idea that maybe there were people who would actually sell his secrets to make money. She wasn't that into sports, but he might be a big enough name that there were people who'd be interested in that information, and she could make money on it.

She supposed assuring him with more words that she would keep her word wasn't really helpful.

In her experience, a person had to back their words up with action, because words that said one thing and actions that said something else made the words worthless.

Right now wasn't the time anyway. They had a contest to not lose.

Chapter Fifteen

Dante hunkered down beside Journee. Obviously, she was fighting her fear pretty hard. It was frustrating to watch and not be able to *do* anything.

"I don't know if it helps or not, but I'm here," he said, looking her straight in the eye.

"It does. Thank you. I feel like I'm being a huge baby." She let out a shaky laugh and looked up. "It feels like it's smaller than it was the last time I did it. But I kind of feel like this is like jumping into a swimming pool. The best thing to do is to just go to the deep end and jump." Still, she didn't move.

"Tell you what, I'll sing a silly song, a really silly Christmas song, nice and loud and deep, so it echoes through the chimney, while you're going up. You can close your eyes, because it'll be dark, and my voice will be right there, right beside you. How's that?"

"You don't have to do that." Although the thought made her smile, and he thought maybe some of the stiffness released from her shoulders.

"It's the least I can do, since you're going first." He winked, and they grinned at each other, sharing a little joke.

She took a breath and stood, and he put his head right down next to her knees, and as she leaned back against one side, pushing herself up, he started to bellow the silliest Christmas song he could think of.

> *"Momma left carrots for Santa Claus,*
> *Along with a tall glass of juice,*
> *She said that dieting would help his cause,*
> *But Dad said he's not a moose..."*

He finished the first verse, totally making it up off the cuff, just as she yelled down, "I'm up. I made it. I've got the flag. Sing some more, because I'm coming down."

So, he made up a second verse to the silliest Christmas song ever.

> *"After my parents went off to bed,*
> *I sneaked down and switched the plate,*
> *Cookies and milk as the songs said,*
> *Coal lumps would not be my fate!"*

Her feet plopped to the ground as he finished.

She ducked under, coming out, all smiles, her cheeks flushed. Her eyes sparkling. "That's a fantastic strategy – make me laugh too hard to feel claustrophobic. Totally worked!"

He stared at her, having to bite back the words to tell her that she was beautiful and brave and hilarious.

Instead, he said, "Of all the people in the world that I could be paired up with in the Not Such an Ironman Ironman Contest, I think you would be my very first pick."

Even that was more than he should have said probably. After the words came out, he ducked under and stood up in the chimney. Climbing up wasn't that hard, although he was definitely on the big side to be squeezing in. Whoever had built the chimney hadn't figured on someone his size being a part of the contest.

Still, he was able to easily grab the flag at the top and scoot back down.

"One down, four to go. I think we've got this," he said, glancing around at the other contestants, none of whom had finished their first task.

"I think we go that direction next," she said, her brows raised, as though making sure.

"I have to admit I wasn't paying a whole lot of attention when he explained everything. There were just so many things that were kinda wild."

"I agree. Still, I think that's where we go."

He nodded. "I'm with you."

They started walking side by side toward the table with all the big boxes of decorations on it. Dante took her hand with what felt like natural ease. She allowed it.

He spoke casually. "So, do you feel like you conquered your current claustrophobia, or was that just a one-time thing?"

"I think, as long as you're singing to me...I might even lock myself in a closet just to hear it."

"Okay. I think the lady is making fun of my poetry skills."

"Isn't that what you do in your spare time? You're a poet?"

"I think that's a skill I just discovered today. But I've got a feeling the football better still come first."

She didn't have a smart retort as he expected. If anything, her face lost a little of its glow.

Was she against football?

That didn't bode well for his chances. He'd deliberately kept from saying anything to her about football in their letters. Maybe they needed to talk about it. He kinda looked a little different than most of the guys in town, a little bigger, but he supposed his status as a pro player hadn't been something he really wore on his sleeve.

Maybe she didn't like being reminded of it.

Or maybe it made her uncomfortable in some way.

That's almost the way it seemed.

"Here's our box," she said, leaning over and looking in, using her hand to move things around. "Oh boy, this could get interesting."

He looked in the box with her, ignoring the calls from the stands. He'd vaguely heard them while they were doing their chimney climbing and especially the cheers once they were done, but now people seemed to be shouting advice at them from where they sat in the stands or stood along the roped-off area.

"Is this where I admit that I've never done a craft voluntarily in my life before? I seem to recall going to some kind of youth activities at the church when I was kid, dragged there by some relative, and being forced to participate in coloring and doing something with scissors. I just want to say I hated it then, and I've never voluntarily picked up a glue gun since. Just throwing that out there." He lifted his shoulder and tried to look manly despite the decorations in front of him.

Journee held up what he considered to be a particularly hideous wall hanging type thing that had red and green feathers and a fuzzy purple outline framing what looked like a pretty good imitation of the Charlie Brown Christmas tree.

"I think ugly Christmas sweaters everywhere are cringing at that particular decoration," he murmured.

"Beauty is in the eye of the beholder," Journee said, with fake-sounding wisdom. "Honestly, for me, the uglier something is, the more I like it. I think it's a pity thing, or maybe it's just I relate to their feelings."

"That is an inanimate object. It doesn't have feelings. I went to college for four years, and despite the fact I played football, they gave me a piece of paper at the end that said I actually learned a little bit of something."

"Maybe they were overly optimistic?" Journee said, obviously joking, but then she pulled a few more decorations out of the boxes. "I wasn't a cute kid. I pretty much had no idea how to comb my hair, and being that I was the youngest, I wore a lot of hand-me-downs. I got teased a lot for my looks, which honestly I didn't always understand since I didn't really know what good things look like, but I think that definitely gave me empathy for ugly things."

"You couldn't have been ugly. No kid is ugly."

"I agree. I guess I don't really think of myself as ugly as much as I think of myself as being perceived as ugly. There's a bit of a difference."

"I agree with that. We can be attuned to what other people think of us, and it affects the way we think of ourselves." He'd been thought of as a pain in the butt and something that people had to deal with. The thoughts of his parents arguing about who had to take him ran through his mind, plus being shuffled around various relatives and friends who would have preferred him not be with them.

Some of them were pretty obvious and dropped him off at someone else's house while they took their "real" children to special events or had family time with just their birth children.

But as Journee shaped the tree and he used the glue gun where she indicated, he figured that she probably just dealt with things slightly different than he did.

Where he took all of those people who didn't want him and replaced them with football, doing his best to excel in that area, she had developed empathy for others who were treated like her.

Even if they were ugly Christmas decorations.

"I'm sorry. I got too serious, and you got quiet," she said, carefully setting a bulb on the line of hot glue he'd squeezed out and holding it there while the glue cooled.

"You don't need to apologize. I was just thinking that probably we both have things in our childhood that shaped us, and where I kind of turned to football, you just developed empathy. Neither one of us were wrong. We handled things differently."

"You got locked in a closet?" Her voice held surprise.

"No. I'm just like a million other kids out there whose parents didn't really want them. That marks a kid." He didn't want to get into the details. They'd been having so much fun he wanted to think of something light and fluffy to talk about.

But her face scrunched up, and that empathy she had for the ugly Christmas decoration was directed at him. He had to admit, better empathy than pity.

"Don't feel bad for me. I can't say it was the best thing that ever happened to me, but I really do think that I wouldn't be a pro ballplayer today if I hadn't had the scrappy childhood I had. It takes a lot of grit to be where I am. Especially since I didn't have a lot of the natural talent a lot of the other guys I play with have. Some of them practice half as much as I do, less even, and it just all comes naturally to them. And then there's me. No matter how much I practice and how well everyone says I do in games, sometimes I feel like I'm just barely above average."

She huffed at that, placing a purple bulb, with what looked like a walrus on it, next to a red one. "I hardly think that you would be a pro ballplayer if you were just barely above average. In fact, from what I'm gathering from listening to other people's conversations, you're actually a pretty big deal."

"You don't watch football, do you?"

"No." Her look was apologetic before she focused back on the hodgepodge of decorations that were slowly forming their way into being shaped like a tree. "Our family was all about cowboys. I could tell you the top guys on the rodeo circuit right now. Actually, Martin would have been one of those fellows that I would have named except he just retired. He's a pretty good bareback bronc rider."

"Retired? He get hurt?"

Her fingers, delicately wrapping a purple thread around the creases in the bulbs—somehow it seemed to blend perfectly with the kaleidoscope of colors—flexed and moved gracefully. He'd never thought of fingers as graceful before.

"I don't think so." She looked over her shoulder as though checking to see where Blakely or Martin were in the crowd of onlookers. "He's not telling anyone, but I kinda got the impression that he was ready to settle down, and he likely found love. And when you love someone, you put them first."

He snorted. There was a lot of derision in that snort that he hadn't really meant to show. "A man can't put anything ahead of his career. You just can't. Even a woman, if she wants to do well, everything else has to come second. I think that's probably why a lot of women aren't in top jobs, not because they can't, but because they put their family first. Men have less trouble doing that."

Her eyes kinda snapped at him, and he knew the whole woman/man thing was a touchy subject. Maybe he shouldn't have said anything, but he felt like it served his point.

"There's nothing wrong with putting your family first. Maybe you should find a different career if you can't manage to make sure that your family knows you love them. Maybe you're right about women doing that more, but I think that makes them smarter."

He held his hands up, the glue gun on one side above his head. "Hey. I didn't want to fight about it. Just saying. That's why men hit the top more often than women. Not because we're smarter, just because we've got that single-minded focus where we put our eyes on where we're going and we don't let anything distract us from it. Including wife and family."

"You can't think that that's a good thing." Her voice held just a touch of disbelief and maybe a little derision.

He dabbed glue right where her finger tapped, and she pressed a piece of shimmering lace that would serve as garland, apparently, on it.

"It's a good thing if you want to be successful in the business world."

"Aren't families more important?"

Chapter Sixteen

$\mathcal{D}$ante knew he was pushing the limits. He weighed his words carefully. "I think people are important. But I think sometimes a man's family knows that they had to make certain sacrifices if that means he's going to be successful."

She pressed her lips together and nodded, but he wasn't fooled. She didn't agree with him.

He could explain further, but he'd be digging a deeper hole for himself, because he knew if he had a wife and kids, his wife and kids would take up his time and attention and focus, and he wouldn't be able to put all of himself into practicing and training and studying and memorizing and getting better.

He wouldn't be as good as what he was if he had to give more of his attention to someone else than to football. And it wasn't just football, it was anything that anyone wanted to excel at. They had to work toward it with a single-minded focus.

"Maybe that's why I'm not married."

"I'm sure that there are ballplayers who are."

"You're right." He ran through some of them in his head, more convinced than ever that he was right.

Once they got married, their focus wasn't on football a hundred percent even when they were at camp, in practice, and of course in games, at least most of the time.

"I do a lot of work outside of practice and games. When I say I live football, I mean it. Maybe some guys don't have to be quite as diligent and they'd still be good. It just wouldn't work for me."

"So you're not getting married."

"I didn't say that." He could hardly say if he wanted a woman; he was looking at the woman who would be his first and only pick. He hadn't been doing a very good job of convincing her to be with him. But he also couldn't pretend to be something other than what he was. It wasn't fair. Not when he was looking for a serious commitment. "I just need to find a woman who understands."

"I see."

He searched his brain for something to make his position look better to her. When he came up with a blank on that, he tried to think of something to change the subject, because obviously what they were talking about wasn't something they were going to agree on.

It didn't make him like her any less, but he had a feeling that her opinion of him was going downhill. And fast.

"Okay, let me ask you this. I'm not saying that you're wrong that a family should come first. That just makes sense. I was neglected as kid, and I pretty much agree with that. But in order to be successful, you have to put everything into what you do. Right?"

She lifted a shoulder, digging through the box for another bulb. "I agree. The more time you devote to something, the more successful you'll probably be."

"Women admire success in a man. They do. They admire a man who's at the top. Are you telling me that after they marry him, they want him to stop doing what it was that they admired and that attracted them to him in the first place, and they would prefer that he be less successful in order to spend more time with them?"

She held the Christmas tree up, looking it over, before digging in the box and finding a cylinder type ornament, which she set about attaching as the base of the Christmas tree, speaking as she adjusted it. "I see your point. I suppose if that's what attracted her in the first place, then it would almost be like false advertising or deceit if you were to change."

"False advertising. I kinda like that."

She chuckled. "Sometimes, I think of makeup as false advertising. That's how Blakely always described it anyway." There was obvious affection in her voice when she talked about her sister.

"I take it you don't share her sentiments?" She was most definitely wearing makeup.

"I see what she's saying. I guess I got teased so much when I was younger though, I always felt like I need all the help I can get."

"I think you'd be just fine with no 'help.' And I think I might agree with Blakely. Sometimes, it's kind of shocking to see the way a woman really looks versus the way she looks when you're out on a date." He'd certainly been shocked more than once.

"Oh, that's right, I forgot you mentioned something about that yesterday. You're like the date expert."

"You gonna hold it against me for the rest of my life? So yeah, I've been on a lot of dates. Had a lot of girlfriends…"

"No. I promise. I won't hold it against you for the rest of your life. I'll respect your experience, and if I ever have any questions about dating, I know who I can ask."

"You sure can. Ask away." He glued a bit of brown tatting to the slender ornament she had as the stem.

"Think this'll do it."

"Is it going to need to stand by itself? Do we need to make a stand for it?"

"Oh. I didn't think about that." She scrunched her brows together while he looked in the box, digging a little with his hand before he found a decoration that was shaped similar to a spider. It would make a perfect stand for the tree.

"I'm not even sure what this is, but I think it'll work."

"I think you're right. We can take some glitter from this." She pulled a sparkling wall hanging out. "And decorate that to make it look a little prettier, not so plain."

She proceeded to do exactly what she'd said, and he had to admit the effect was striking.

He unplugged the glue gun from the extension cord lying on the ground, and they both stepped back away from the table.

"There. For a minute, I really didn't think it was possible, but you made that tree look gorgeous. If we lose, it's not going to be because of the tree."

She glowed, looking up at him. "Thank you."

"I'm glad my choice of topics didn't distract you and didn't affect your ability to decorate."

"You know what, I think it's okay for us to disagree. I really do. There's no law that says that friends have to agree on everything. And sometimes, I think even though I'm pretty sure my way is right, intelligent people disagree all the time, so what makes me so sure that I can't be wrong?"

"That's refreshing. So many times, we're sure we're right, and we can't stand people who disagree with us."

"It just makes sense. It's okay for everyone to be different. I guess the only exception is people who want to disagree with God. You know, that's kinda dumb. In that case, we really don't have to understand, because there's a lot of things that we'll probably never comprehend, but if God says something, that's the final word. It doesn't matter what we think."

"What about when science proves God wrong?" He didn't know why he was picking on her today. He should have just agreed with her and kept his mouth shut.

They took one last look at the Christmas tree and started walking on down to the gift-wrapping area before she answered.

"What about the times when science proves itself wrong? Things we think we know, and then they change."

"Like what?"

"Well, just a silly example," she said. "When I was growing up, my mom claimed that margarine was healthier than butter. That's what 'science' told us. And now, we know that's not the case. It changed. You know? There's lots of things like that. I mean come on, we used to think that leeches helped people heal. Thank goodness we figured that one out. But there's so many things we don't know and so many things we're discovering, if something seems to prove the Bible wrong, I would question it. Because there have been so many times where scientists claimed the Bible was wrong, and it turns out that science was wrong."

He walked along beside her, quietly. Maybe he didn't say anything, because he could think of plenty of things in the exercise and weightlifting world where things the experts had thought worked later turned out to not work or at least not as well.

"Have I offended you again? Is this another area where we have to agree to disagree?"

"No. Actually, I was thinking about different things I know of where you're exactly right. Things we used to think were right that we eventually figured out aren't true."

"Really? So this is an area where we agree?"

"I think so."

"That's great. I wonder if we should find something that we can argue about though, because I think the Christmas tree turned out pretty well, and maybe we just, you know, do well when we're dealing with some controversy."

He laughed. "That's definitely an interesting way to look at it. Maybe we should experiment, see how well we do whenever we're agreeing on something."

Chapter Seventeen

It turned out they didn't have too much time to talk.

When they got to the gift-wrapping station, there was an attendant at the table, Malley Stern, and she held the jar out from which they could choose the slip of paper which would tell them what gift they were to wrap.

"Someone already got the tricycle. That was one of the hardest." She snapped her gum. "But the hardest by far is still in there. Choose wisely," she said, her eyes blinking as she lifted her brows.

Journee glanced at Dante. "You do the honors?"

"You go ahead. I can't take the pressure."

"That's fine." She shifted her neck to the left with a satisfying crack, then looked back at him. "I can."

He laughed at her giddiness, and she stuck her hand in the jar, pulling out a slip of paper. What could be harder than a tricycle?

Holding the paper up, she closed her eyes for a moment, hoping that she'd misread. She looked at the paper again.

"That look doesn't bode well."

"No." Her lips flattened, and she looked up at him. "It doesn't."

"What do we have? A porcupine?" Dante said in a tone that said he didn't think whatever it was could be too bad.

"A greased pig. We're supposed to wrap a greased pig."

"Can you say pie target?"

"That's exactly what I was thinking. I'm gonna request chocolate cream."

"Oh, don't do that. You'll never get the chocolate stains out of your clothes. You want to wear something nice since you don't want to get up in front of everybody looking ratty," Malley said. Then she looked Journee up and down. "You do have slightly better taste than your sister."

Her loopy earrings bobbled in her ears as she snapped her gum again. Long chains of necklaces roped around her neck, and her shirt was tied in a knot at the bottom, showing just a slice of midsection over her short jean skirt.

Her bracelets jingled as she lifted an arm and indicated a small pen behind her. "Your pig's back there. He's a cute little thing if I do say so myself." Her bracelets jingled again as she swiped an arm over the table in front of her. "Pick your color paper, grab your scissors, and the tape's there too." Her long lashes wiggled at Dante. "If you need me to hold your hand, technically I'm not allowed, but I'll make an exception for you."

Normally, Journee would have laughed, because Malley flirted with everyone. But for some reason, she didn't find it funny today. Maybe because of the looming specter of the chocolate cream pies, but she kinda doubted it. It was probably something a little bit more low class and catty. Something she really didn't like in herself.

She smiled at Malley anyway. "Thanks for the instructions."

"Sorry about your luck," she said, not sounding sorry at all.

"Do you have a preference on color?" Journee asked Dante, looking at the three rows of wrapping paper that were left.

"I think I'd better. Since I allowed you to choose the gift, and it's hard for me to imagine something worse than trying to wrap a greased pig."

"I thought porcupine sounded pretty hard actually. Nice guess, anyway."

"Yeah, it was, wasn't it? Hard to think of anything harder."

"A blue whale, maybe?"

"Oh yeah. I guess anything from the water. It could get messy."

"Good point. Slime might be hard to wrap. Or a bus."

"Shh," he said, looking around. "Don't give them any ideas for next year."

She grabbed the tape and scissors. "Why? You think you're going to be around next year for this?"

"Possibly. I'm actually having fun."

"You sound surprised. I take it you weren't expecting to enjoy this?"

He chose the black paper with gold stars, and one side of his lips lifted up. "No. Honestly, I really wasn't. But I'm not sure it's the contest that's so much fun."

He met her eyes. She wasn't sure exactly what he was saying, but he held them for longer than necessary. Finally, he shifted away and looked at Malley. "Thanks for your help."

"No problem, sweetie. You guys holler when you're done, I gotta snap a picture of that one, 'cause he's not gonna stay in his wrapping long enough for the judges to get a good look."

"Thanks. We'll let you know," Journee said as she followed Dante around to the little pen.

"I think we need to do this kind of quickly. I feel like we're gonna need to make up some time and finish ahead because there's no way that our wrap job is going to be anything but slapdash here." He spoke as they walked.

"Agreed." She didn't have time to say anything more though, because a rumbling noise interrupted them.

They looked up to see a pickup zipping across the field between where the saws were and the copse of trees where they were to cut one down.

"I think they're cheating," Dante said with wonder in his voice. "I can't believe it. Blatantly cheating."

"Well," Journee said thoughtfully, running back over in her mind exactly what Mr. Albright had said the rules were. "Mr. Albright said that if he didn't forbid it, we could do it. He never said we had to actually walk to get the trees."

There was a silence as Dante stood with his mouth hanging open, staring at her, his eyes a million miles away as he seemed to run through what she'd said and probably try to remember exactly what Mr. Albright had told them.

"You're right. He didn't say that. But we're not allowed to leave the course," he added. "So it's not like I can go get my truck and drive us down."

"No," she drew the word out, thinking, her eyes scanning the crowd.

"Journee! Journee! Hey, over here!" Journee turned, recognizing Blakely's voice.

She raised a hand to wave, and Blakely hollered across the tape, "Got you covered." She pointed to the field, and then to Dante and Journee, and back to the field.

Journee grinned and gave a thumbs-up then turned to Dante. "Looks like Blakely's gonna get us a ride. Gotta say, sisters come in handy sometimes."

"I guess they would."

His words were right, but his tone held a thread of something that made Journee turn her head and remember what he had said about his upbringing and his family and the things he'd gone through, and it made her heart hurt a little for him.

But then she remembered what he'd said about it making him a better person and that he was successful in his career because of it. She thought about taking the bad and making it for good.

"How much longer are you going to play pro ball?"

"That question came out of nowhere."

"I'm sorry. I guess I was just thinking that you would make a really great motivational speaker. You know, how hard work and determination can take something that's bad and turn it into something that's really phenomenal. I don't know much about football, but I do know that only a very elite few make it to the top as you have. Considering where you started, it could be really inspiring."

His smile was bright if a little doubtful. "Thanks. I never thought of it, but I appreciate that."

She laughed. "Now I'm thinking we gotta take this bad thing—the pig and wrapping it—and turn it into a win somehow." She threw her arms up. "I'm coming up with a blank. Unless the judges give us credit for effort, I'm pretty sure any kind of wrap job we do on this thing is not going to be great, and, like Malley said, won't last long."

"I have to agree. I guess we'll just do our best. You want to hold the pig, or do you want me to?"

"Do you have any experience holding pigs?" she asked, assuming she knew the answer.

His grin was a little sly. "I'm not going to insult any of my teammates that way."

She huffed out a laugh. "Never even thought of that. I have to say I've held pigs before but none that were greased. That one looks really slippery."

"But cute too."

"I think pigs are about the cutest babies ever."

"All baby animals are cute."

"No one is going to disagree on that one."

"Finally. Something we agree on. See? It wasn't that hard. It only took us," he grabbed his phone out of his pocket and took a glance at it, "ninety minutes," he said, shoving it back in his pocket.

"Not bad. At this rate, we'll have at least three things we agree on by the end of the week."

"We better get a move on it, because I'll be leaving tomorrow."

"Oh?"

"Training camp."

Her heart sank. She knew he wasn't staying. It disappointed her more than she expected, but that just emphasized to her that the fun she was having was fun with a friend. Nothing more.

He didn't notice how his words had affected her, as he said, "I think I'd better hold it, and you'd better wrap it. I've never held a pig before, but I've never wrapped a gift either, so I'm probably bad at both. I'm guessing you've wrapped before at least so that leaves the pig for me."

"You never wrapped a gift before?"

"Nope." He swung a leg over the fence which was not very high.

The pig was small, less than twenty pounds, and cute as a button too. She hadn't been joking about how adorable baby pigs were.

That wasn't what held her attention, though. With the way Dante was acting, he didn't want to talk about it, but she could hardly let it slide.

"You've never wrapped a single gift?"

"Said I didn't," he said, walking toward the pig, leaning over a little, with a hand out.

She felt compelled to say, "Be careful, they'll bite. Watch your fingers."

"Really? This tiny little thing will bite?"

"Yeah. You don't want to have an infected pig bite on your hand. I don't know if you have anything to do with handling the ball at your position, whatever that is, but you definitely don't want an infection in your fingers if you do."

"I do actually." He looked up, humor in his eyes. "Handle the ball, that is. At my position." The humor in his eyes said he found her words funny, and she was a little embarrassed. Maybe she'd said something really dumb, but she wouldn't know.

"If it makes you feel any better, I've never played football. So, maybe that's just as weird as you never wrapping a gift?"

She didn't really think so. Who didn't wrap gifts? At least one?

"I don't know about that, but once I'm able to get my hands on this hog, I should be a little better at keeping hold of it…although typically when I carry the football, it doesn't move." He crept a little closer to the pig. "Plus, they've never greased it as far as I know. I'm pretty sure that's against the rules."

"The ball probably gets slippery in the rain," Journee said as he crept a little closer, bending down even more.

The pig looked at him, unafraid.

Dante closed the last distance fast. Journee thought for sure he had the animal caught, but the pig squealed and darted away at the last second, slipping through his hands. Dante ended up on his knees with empty hands and a bewildered look on his face.

"I think that might be a two-person job," Journee said as she set the scissors and tape down and swung a leg over the fence.

"I think you may be right." Dante looked at his hands before brushing them down his legs and getting to his feet. "They didn't skimp on the grease either. Just saying."

"Thanks. I'll keep that in mind. I think we should get extra credit, because I don't think anyone else actually had to catch their gift before they wrapped it."

"Good point. One we need to point out to the judges."

"Agreed, because I'm pretty sure we're not going to make up any time on this."

"You're right." His words sounded muffled like he was concentrating hard on something else. "You calling this play?" he asked as he crept a little closer.

"That's strategy, right? You're asking me about strategy?"

"You're the farm girl."

"My dad's a pastor. I'm not a farm girl."

"You're closer to it than I am. I live in the city. You know, apartment buildings, cement, skyscrapers? Lots of people, no pens, no pigs." He looked around her. "We're on your turf now."

"Oh my goodness." She thought he was serious. Like she was going to tell him how to catch the pig. Like she had any experience catching greased hogs.

Right. Well, she'd make something up, she supposed. "I think we need to corner him. And then come at him from both sides, and you stop him, and I'll grab him. Or vice versa."

He slowly straightened, putting a hand on his hip. "That's it. That's your play?"

"What?"

"Nothing," he said, and it sounded like "something."

"So…" She'd watched a popular movie about a football player less than a year ago… She tried to think of how they called the plays. She cleared her throat and said in a falsely male voice, "Fifty-five, belly up, nine, five, two, Jack down, pie corner one." She spit in her hand, tapped her nose, stroked her ear, slapped her thigh, and then put both of her hands out toward him one on top of the other. "Let's go!" she said in her best imitation-football-breaking-the-huddle voice.

The corners of his lips twitched, although he tried to keep a stern look on his face.

He pursed his lips a little and looked away as though getting a hold of himself before he looked back at her. "I think you were mocking me."

"No." She opened innocent eyes wide. "Not at all. I was calling a play."

"Oh. You were calling a play?" He nodded, his hands on his hips, looking away again, getting the quick twitching of his lips under control. "That's what that was?"

"Yeah. I thought it was fairly obvious."

"Okay. So," he drew the word out, his eyes shifting to the pig. He'd been looking at her like she was just as crazy as she felt, in a humorous kind of way that made her feel like they were sharing a joke.

He looked back at her. "What exactly are we doing?"

"We're going to catch the pig."

He pressed his lips together, nodding. "Right."

She grinned at him and walked forward, her eyes on the hog. "I think you better catch him, because you've got the good hands."

"I have good hands? Who told you that?"

"You did. Didn't you say you never drop the football?"

"I think you've been checking up on me. Because I never said that."

"Then it's true?"

"Yeah. Pretty much." His look was sheepish, like he didn't want to brag about his record, but she was pretty sure she'd heard someone say that. She really hadn't looked him up. Although, it wasn't a bad idea.

"Good. I'll chase him; you catch him." They both walked toward the corner and the piglet, who eyed them with a little more trepidation than he had the first time.

"I think he's wising up," Dante said softly.

"I was getting that impression, too," Journee said. "We'd better catch him the first time, otherwise he'll be even smarter the next time we get him cornered."

"You speaking from experience? Or are you just making this up on the fly?"

"Don't you improvise plays in the middle?"

"Coach gets a little upset when we do that."

"Not if it works out."

"Actually, sometimes we take flak even when it works out."

"Well, let's stick to the play, but if things go sideways in the middle, we'll improvise. And the coach won't be giving you any flak."

"So now you're the coach?" he asked as they crept forward another foot.

"I thought that's why I was calling the play?"

"That makes you the quarterback. Or whatever the pig-catching equivalent is of a quarterback."

"I don't think there is an equivalent. I'm pretty sure there's no comparison between football and catching a hog. I could be wrong."

"We'll have to Google it."

She laughed. "I don't have a computer."

Chapter Eighteen

_D_ante stopped, and Journee took his shocked look to be because she didn't have a computer.

Typical.

She held a hand up, careful not to scare the hog with any quick movements. "I know. I know. Totally unusual in today's day and age, but I do have a smartphone, and I know how to use it."

He jerked his head, looking back at the pig, focused again on their task.

She could kick herself. Normal people had computers. Of course, she knew people thought she was weird when she admitted that she didn't. She should have known better.

"Sorry. Now I feel awkward. Like you think I'm a freak."

"No," he said, way too quickly. "I don't."

"Right. That definitely sounded like a 'you're a total nutjob, and I want to get as far away from you as possible.' It's okay. You don't have to deny it. I'm kinda used to it."

"Why don't you have a computer?" he asked instead. Not denying anything that she'd said, and she kind of felt like he agreed with it but didn't want to hurt her feelings.

"I don't know. I guess I just want to be different."

"Try again."

"Time suck?"

"I believe that. What else?"

"I don't need one. I don't want one. And I don't want to be bothered with one. I'm happy with what I am, and I don't need to go online to have some kind of alternate personality."

"What about shopping?"

"I go to the store." She shrugged. Just a little because they were awfully close to the pig and she didn't want to scare it. "But I don't really like to shop."

He froze again, and she had the feeling that this time he really did think she was a crackpot. "A woman who doesn't like to shop?"

"I think we should get it on the count of three. One, two—"

"Wait."

She had her mouth open to start the word three before she turned her head. "What?"

"I've never met a woman who didn't like to shop. That's so weird."

"I know. I know. We already had this conversation. I'm weird. Everyone knows it. Let's catch the pig." She looked back at the animal who was staring at them like they were nuts. "Three!"

She charged forward.

She had to hand it to him, his reflexes were fast. He went from shocked consternation, staring at her, to almost catching the pig.

It slipped through his hands again and ran to the far side of the little pen.

They lined up again without saying anything, and that time, when she moved on the hog, he was down in a crouch—she might say a good defensive lineman position, but she really wasn't sure—and when the pig came at him, he grabbed a hind leg and didn't let go.

The pig squealed a bit, but Dante immediately started petting it under the chin, which caused it to calm down quite nicely, but he looked at her with what looked like panic on his face.

"Now what do we do? And do you really think it will bite me?"

"I'm really not a pig expert, so I couldn't say for sure, but I'm impressed you caught him. If that means anything."

"So..." He raised his brows, waiting.

She looked back, raising her brows too.

"Are...you...gonna wrap the pig here?"

She'd wrapped plenty of gifts, but none in a pen. "Yes?" "Can you do it on your own?"

"Okay," she said like he hadn't asked it as a question. She had no clue.

He bit his lip, laughing and rolling his eyes at the same time.

She pulled her phone from her pocket and pull up the camera app. "Smile."

"Seriously. No. You are not taking my picture."

"Oh yes, I am. I'm going to post this as blackmail somewhere. Guaranteed."

She snapped it with his mouth hanging open. "Now, would you like me to take one with you smiling?"

"You are joking. Seriously."

"No way. I think I'll caption the picture 'good hands.' What do you think?"

"I think maybe you'd better get the pig wrapped before I lose it. We can talk about the picture later." He shifted, hunkering down and continuing to scratch the piglet's chin. "Or maybe you can just give me one for my own blackmailing scheme."

She'd already scrambled across the fence, grabbed the paper, scissors, and tape, called up to Malley to be ready to snap a pic, and scurried back over the fence.

"I think you'd be pretty hard-pressed to find an incriminating picture like that for me. Not to mention, you'd be even more hard-pressed to find anybody who cares about an incriminating picture like that with me. You, on the other hand, seem to have somewhat of the following, plus all those old girlfriends who will probably get a great kick out of it, and how could I resist?"

"Easily. Let me help you resist. It's like this. 'I don't want to take a picture of the football player.'"

"That's not true. You look so adorable holding that hog, plus with your great hands, it makes a good pic."

She wasn't exactly sure, but he seemed to know that she was completely joking, although she really had snapped the picture. Just because he was funny.

She scrunched up her nose. "Suggestions on how to wrap this thing?"

"I've never wrapped anything, remember?"

"That's right. If you and I spend any more time together, you are definitely getting gift-wrapping lessons. A person cannot go through life never having wrapped a gift. And I'm not even kidding about that."

"Will you hate me if I say I can think of about seven thousand things I would rather do other than wrap gifts?"

"Of course not. I never thought for one second that you actually wanted to wrap anything. But we learn all kinds of things we don't actually want to do, right? Like cook? You have to cook, right?"

"Takeout."

"You're kidding."

"No. Why would I want to know how to cook?"

She didn't quite believe him with the twinkle in his eye, but she went with his words and not her gut feeling. "So that you don't have to eat takeout."

"Takeout can be healthy. I mean you know you can get healthy takeout. The grocery store down the street lets you buy salad by the pound, and you can make it however you want to."

She shook her head. "Stop. Just stop. You don't wrap gifts, you can't cook...what can you do?"

He looked at his hands. "Apparently, I can catch hogs."

He lifted the leg that he still held and continued to scratch the piglet. The piglet kind of acted like it wanted to lie down.

"If you put that thing asleep, I'll be really impressed."

"I'm doing my best. I think his eyes are closed. If it's sleeping while standing on three legs, that counts, right?"

"It has to be lying down in order for it to count. Nice try though." She pursed her lips, blowing out through them, studying the pig. She had no idea how to wrap something that was going to be moving.

The artist in her balked at the idea, but she said, "I think the best thing to do is to just get a lot of paper out and wrap it up like a blanket with as much paper as we can get on it, throw pieces of tape on it to keep it stuck, and yell for Malley."

"You're calling the play again."

She laughed. "No. But I can if you want me to."

He shook his head. "No, you're gonna say something like Hicks twenty-five slant back J through one. You'll just end up confusing everyone."

"Considering that everyone is exactly you and the pig, I don't think that that's the worst thing that could happen here."

"You could be right about that. I can think of several other things that could happen that could be worse than being confused." He looked at his hand and seemed to judge the short distance between his hand and the backside spigot on the pig.

Journee had to giggle. "It might be worse for you, but the only thing that could make my original picture better would be to have some additional...organic matter in it."

"Organic matter sounds like a rather erudite term for something that could more basely be termed—"

Journee put her hand up. "This is a family festival."

"I was gonna say poop."

She narrowed her eyes at his innocent look. "Sorry. My bad," she said sweetly.

Taking the wrapping paper, she did exactly what she said she was going to do—unrolled it, held it over the pig, and wrapped the tube around and around and around.

"You do realize you have my hand in that?"

"Was there a rule against that? I mean, was I not allowed to wrap hands along with the gifts?"

His face scrunched a little, thinking. "I guess not."

"Well then, consider it your sacrifice for The Cause."

"I'm kind of feeling like I should be getting a movie vibe here, but I'm not."

"That doesn't surprise me. I was totally channeling *Gone With the Wind*, but I don't think it's politically correct anymore anyway, so you're probably very hip to be completely clueless."

"Well, it's important to me to be hip, so I'll continue to be clueless."

Journee groaned without taking her eyes off her work. "I'm getting ready to put the tape on. You want to call Malley? She seemed like she was more partial to you than me anyway."

"Think so?" There was definitely humor in his voice, and she was sure he knew exactly what she was talking about.

He called Malley's name while Journee taped the top of the pig and around the back, taping the actual paper to his arm and shrugging her shoulders at his hey-what-are-you-doing look.

"I don't think you can let go of it, and I don't want to cut your arm off, I'm guessing that's against the rules, so this is the third best thing."

"Nice. Cutting my arm off was an actual consideration. It's not looking good for your non-serial-killer prospects."

"Hey, you'll come visit me, right?"

"In prison? As long as they have you in a straitjacket."

"Doesn't sound like you two are getting along too well if you want to see her put in a straitjacket." Malley sashayed over to the rail. "What's she doing to you, sweetheart? You should have requested a partner that would be a little nicer to you." Malley put a slim hand over the edge of the fence, her bright red nail polish glistening in the sun.

Whether the pig was just getting tired of having his chin rubbed, or whether he didn't like Malley's voice, Journee wasn't sure, but he started to wiggle and grunt. One sharp little hoof pushed through the bottom of the paper.

Journee was going to suggest, sweetly of course, that Malley swing a leg over and come on in, but she eyed the miniskirt and decided that she'd better not.

"I think Dante would really appreciate it if you take the picture fast."

"I don't know about that. He looks like he's strong enough to handle a little piglet."

"I don't think it's about being strong, Malley. I think it's more about the pig is slippery and it's started to move. Take the picture."

"Smile, Dante." Malley held her phone in her hand, looking over it, waiting for Dante to comply.

He did, almost immediately, because the pig was struggling for real, and Journee was sure he was hoping he would be able to keep it still long enough for Malley to get the camera app up and focused.

"Hurry up, Malley, I'm losing it."

"Don't you worry about a thing, Dante. I can help you hold it together."

"Talking about the pig," Dante grunted, just before the animal slipped out of his grasp, slid under the bottom fence rail, where the paper caught and mostly slipped off his body, except for a piece that he'd apparently been chewing on, unbeknownst to everyone, and that trailed behind him as he streaked between Malley's legs and took off toward the hot sausage stand two hundred yards away.

Journee figured he'd have been smarter to head for the cactus fries, but she hadn't been asked her opinion.

Malley screeched and jumped up on the fence, dropping her phone and holding on to the post, looking traumatized.

Journee watched the pig as it ran across the field, dodging

people, trailing wrapping paper, until finally two teen girls in jeans and boots looking for all the world like they wrestled hogs all the time jumped on it with one of them capturing both hind legs, one in each hand, and picking it up.

"Someone caught it," she said, looking down at Dante who had landed on his butt and was sitting with legs bent, both forearms braced on them, and an annoyed look on his face which had traces of amusement as he met her eyes.

She looked over at Malley, who was still up on the second rung of the fence, clutching the post, although thankfully not screeching anymore.

"Did you get a picture?" she asked, trying to keep her tone calm and not sound like she was desperately hoping that she had.

"No."

"Really? You didn't get even one?" Dante asked, not exactly yelling but definitely frustrated. She'd been standing there for a long time.

"No. I was waiting for you to smile. I'm sure you didn't want me to take the picture with you looking like a big old grouch. This could be on the front page of the local paper. It's a big deal."

"Pretty sure he'd have been fine with a picture and no smile," Journee murmured, not looking at Dante, because she thought, while she didn't exactly feel irritated, he did.

After all, he was the one sitting on his butt in the dirt right now. With no picture and grease on his hands. At least he hadn't gotten bitten.

She looked down at him, her brows raised, the expression on her face saying, "what can we do, right?"

"How do you feel about banana cream?" he asked.

Chapter Nineteen

Thankfully by the time the girls brought the pig back, most of the grease was rubbed off of it, and Dante didn't have such a hard time holding it while Journee wrapped it quickly and efficiently. It was the third time, after all.

Malley snapped the picture, and he only growled at her twice.

Actual growling. Which, of course, made Journee give him a quelling look.

He was pretty sure though that, for the most part, she was having a good time. Even if their prospects for not getting pies in the face were pretty small.

Microscopic.

But it was okay. It was more important to have fun.

He might not have started the day believing that, but he was ending it that way. Or at least living it that way.

They should save some time with Blakely making sure they got a ride down to the Christmas tree. All they had to do was cut it down, and her ride would get them there and back.

Almost made him wish he had siblings.

"So what kind of ride does Blakely have?" he asked, scanning the area where an older couple was just getting out of their golf cart and grabbing their tree off the back.

He was thinking a Jeep or a pickup—Blakely seemed like the type—but he'd take a golf cart.

"Um...how severe was that phobia that you mentioned earlier?" Journee asked, very hesitantly.

Her tone made his eyes slash to hers, and he noted the crinkling of her brows and the way she bit her lip.

Actually, he got a little distracted by the way she bit her lip.

He hadn't impressed her, hadn't done anything that might make her choose to be with him, other than maybe make her laugh.

Still, he was almost certain that it would be better in the long run if he didn't lie to her, or deceive her, or let her think for one second that he was something he wasn't or that football wasn't going to be the most important thing in his life, during the season at least.

It had to be.

Obviously, she didn't like that. He didn't know any player's wife who liked that.

Part of him hoped she'd choose him anyway, and part of him thought that he'd gotten along without a family so far throughout his life, so he didn't really need one.

He thought about being in the hospital and the fear of being alone.

And part of him thought that the game wasn't going to last forever, and maybe he should work on building something that would.

"Are you thinking? Or did you forget the question?" Journee asked, snapping his attention back to the present.

"Phobia. Horse." His eyes narrowed as comprehension began to dawn. "Why are you asking?"

"Because Blakely's ride for us...is a horse." Her face expressed concern, but she also bounced a little on her toes, like she was kind of in a hurry. And he got that. The couple who got done first wasn't necessarily the winner, but they were almost guaranteed to not be the loser. And since that was pretty much all they had going for them at the present time, he got the rush.

Although she had made a nice Christmas tree out of the ornaments.

"You're kidding," he said, even though he knew she wasn't. It was Blakely, after all, and even though he'd only met her a couple of times, he should have known that she would have provided a horse. "What about the golf cart? Do you think we could borrow it?"

Journee looked over, but she was already shaking her head. The golf cart was being driven away by a kid who looked like he was about five. "I'm pretty sure they're not going to share."

"Seriously? Is this a Christian festival? Maybe now would be a really good time for a short sermon on biblical communication."

The worry on Journee's face melted away into a grin. "I'm impressed. You used the biblical term for sharing."

"Sunday School. Some of those lessons are hard to forget."

"I'm sure that's probably the way they meant it. All the cookies and juice they fed you had a tendency to make things stick."

"Bribe the kids with food. Is that a universal Christian thing? Is that a verse in the Bible they didn't have us memorize?"

"The Bible does do an awful lot of talking about food. So, maybe." Her face scrunched again. "Should we jog?"

He judged the distance to the copse of trees. It was pretty far. Then his gaze went back to the horse.

"I thought you said Blakely did trick riding? Isn't this like a high-dollar horse? Could we hurt it?"

"No. I don't think Blakely would ever let anyone ride Candy or Kisses. But she and Martin have several other horses they're training, and this is one of those."

"So this is like a half-broke horse?"

"Isn't that a book?" Journee said, totally distracted from the subject at hand.

"Focus." He waited for her eyes to meet his. "Am I going to fall off the horse? Or is it going to do something else that will hurt?"

"I don't think so," Journee said in a tone that did not convince him of anything other than the fact that he probably *was* going to fall off.

"Could you say that in a little more reassuring tone and maybe add a blood promise on the end of that. It would make me feel better."

"How about I just sing a silly Christmas song? That's what I got while facing my phobia?"

"Really? How about the whole do-unto-others thing? You know, act with your Christian beliefs instead of throwing my faults and failures in my face every time we disagree."

"So, we have a double standard. I get silly songs, and you want promises."

"You know what. Never mind. I'll ride the horse. And you don't even have to sing."

"That's a good thing. We want the horse to stay calm and in good mood. If I start to sing, I can only see bad things happening."

"It can't be that bad."

"It's that bad."

They'd walked over to where Blakely was holding the horse behind the starting line and really not paying attention as she seemed to be communicating with Martin who still stood behind the yellow tape.

Blakely jerked her head around as Journee walked up.

"Thanks so much, sis. I really appreciate it. This is so much better than jogging." Journee gave Dante an eye and kinda nodded her head like encouraging him to say something along similar lines.

He tried to think of something he could say that wouldn't be a total lie. "I think this is probably going to be faster than jogging." Unless he fell off and broke his other leg. Maybe he shouldn't ride the horse at all, but then he'd be letting Journee down. He usually didn't have this much trouble making up his mind, but he felt like he was wavering back and forth, because he truly was scared of horses.

Journee leaned toward him and looked up.

"Face your fear?" she said, low so that only he could hear as he leaned his head down.

"Did I say this was a phobia? I meant allergy. I'm deathly allergic to horses."

"Nice try. I can get on first, if you're good riding behind me." She lifted her brows. "Or do you want to be in the front?"

"If I'm in the front that means I have to steer, right?"

"Steer. Yes. That's what you have to do if you're in front. Steer. Like a ship. Or a car. Only there's no wheel. You've got reins."

"Quit making fun of me. I didn't make fun of you whenever you were trying to go up the chimney."

"I didn't say anything about steering when I went up the chimney."

"Right. Got it. Some of us didn't grow up in the country. What do you say whenever you're going to steer a horse?"

"Can we talk about this later? Can't we just get on the horse?"

"Ladies first."

Journee nodded, giving him a worried glance, but she also seemed to be biting back a smile. She grabbed the mane, did something weird with her other hand too quickly for him to quite catch at all, and before he knew it, she jumped up, throwing her leg over, and was suddenly astride the horse.

"I'm sorry. But I don't think there's any way I'm going to be able to get on from the ground," Dante said to no one in particular or to everyone. He wasn't sure.

Journee's lips pursed, and she and Blakely exchanged glances. Blakely checked her watch. "I don't want to put pressure on anyone, but you guys are pretty much in last place right now. Even the grandparents are ahead of you."

"It's okay. I dealt with some claustrophobia on the chimneys, and that's probably what got us behind."

"No. I've been dragging my feet about the horse. How about you tell me what to do to get on." Dante started walking toward the horse. He could do this. He'd done plenty of hard things in his life before.

Blakely and Journee exchanged another look before Journee patted the sleek neck and said, "If I walk the horse over to the table, do you mind climbing up on the table and slipping onto his back from there?"

Dante didn't answer her but strode to the table. Hopefully, he got this over with before anybody could snap a picture, because this was definitely something his teammates would make fun of him for for pretty much the rest of his career. He could see this picture ending up both in the locker room and also on national TV.

Blakely didn't hesitate. She rode the horse over behind him.

He felt like an idiot as he climbed up on the table, but he had to admit she was right—it made it a lot easier for him to slip onto the horse.

Maybe he was clutching Journee's waist a little tighter than necessary, but he felt like he was gonna fall off at any second.

"Relax."

"Tell the horse to Stop. Moving. And I will relax."

"The point of having the horse is to have it move," Journee said, explaining it almost like he was five and she were teaching him how to write the first letter of his name.

"Right. I knew that." It just felt like he needed to catch his balance before it started moving more. "Go ahead. I'm ready." He seriously felt he was going to fall off at any second, which made him tense and squeeze. He was holding on pretty tight. "Can you breathe?"

"Not really. But if we go fast, I might make it back here before I pass out."

"Funny."

"Seriously, Dante. I know it's hard to relax, mostly because you're used to being in control. But just try to feel the horse underneath you, and just let your body move with it. As athletic as you are, I know you have great balance. Trust me."

"Trust you? What about the horse?"

"Me. No horse is perfect, but Blakely wouldn't have brought us a horse that was going to be a problem. I'm not the greatest rider in the world, and she knows it."

Her head was turned sideways, and he leaned down, deliberately brushing his cheek with hers and accidentally distracting himself from the idea of the horse.

Maybe he wouldn't say it out loud, but rather than closing his eyes and trusting the horse, maybe he could close his eyes and savor the scent of pine needles and ginger and something else that reminded him of laughter and light and an easy friendship that wanted to be more.

If he hadn't been sitting on the horse with his arms around her, he might have missed the shiver. As it was, it matched his.

His voice lowered. "I'm starting to see the advantages of riding horseback. Keep talking."

"I didn't say anything," she murmured, and he thought maybe she was as distracted as he was by the brush of their skin. "I'm wondering if Blakely planned this."

"I think you belong to a family of matchmakers."

"I think maybe you better consider yourself warned."

"I'm not sure warned is the right word."

She seemed to relax back into him before she tensed. He wanted to ask what the problem was, but she turned her head forward and did something. The horse started walking.

"Are you okay with this?" she asked.

"I am. You can go faster. I'll try not to cut your air off."

"Breathing is overrated. I'll catch up on it tonight. Hold on as tight as you need to."

She wasn't waif thin like a lot of the women he dated had been. There was a sturdiness about her that felt as substantial as her personality and the things she believed. She felt solid and grounded like she was true enough to be an anchor but not unbendable.

Those weren't ever qualities he'd looked for or appreciated in a woman, but his accident and the letters he'd exchanged with Journee had altered his values and he found himself thinking things he'd never considered before.

Everything probably would have been okay if the teenage couple who was competing against them hadn't gone screeching by in a truck that Dante swore did not have a muffler at all.

The sound grew, and it wasn't exactly a shock, but it reached a pitch that the horse could no longer take, and the body under him went from a gentle rock to a jerk, dip, swoop, and then it disappeared from beneath him.

That was the only way he could explain it.

It took a little while for him to get his brain function going as he lay on his back, staring up at the sky, a little dazed as to how he got there.

It wasn't much consolation that Journee lay with her head on his stomach between his legs.

He had a feeling the reason she fell off was because he didn't let go of her.

He was still struggling to breathe, but that thought made him battle to sit up.

"I'm sorry. With all that was happening, it made me clutch tighter rather than loosen my grip. I know you'd still be on that horse if it weren't for me."

He'd managed to sit up, bringing her up too, with his legs bent on either side of Journee, and his arms around her, his face over her shoulder so that when she turned her head, their noses almost touched.

"It's okay. I can't agree with that. I'm not a good rider, especially when a horse bolts like that."

Her breath whispered across his face, and while he heard her words, he was much more interested in watching the movement of her lips. The pain from falling off the horse had almost completely faded from his mind, superseded by the feeling that the woman in his arms was perfectly placed.

The bands of heat shooting out from his chest were new and enjoyable, too.

"Are you okay? I guess that should have been my first question."

"You kind of cushioned my fall."

"Kind of?"

"Yeah. Kind of, because you're hard. And I'm not sure whether it would have been softer to land on the ground or to land on you."

"I think there's a compliment in there somewhere."

"Probably. But I think you're gonna need to dig for it."

"I can do that."

He brought a hand up, pushing her hair away from her face, running his thumb along the line of her jaw, and bending a little closer. "Glad you're okay," he said, wanting to say more but realizing that this was terrible timing.

"Are you?"

"Yeah. I feel like the little bit of pain on my backside right now is completely worth it."

"Pretty sure you're lying."

"No. I'm not." By this time, Blakely had caught the horse and was leading it back, and he didn't have nearly enough time to tell her everything he wanted to, but maybe he shouldn't. He tilted his head just slightly and brushed his lips along her temple.

She stiffened, and he figured he probably moved too fast.

He decided he'd better lighten the mood. "I think I've fallen for you."

He wanted to say it light and teasing and make fun of the fact that they'd just fallen off the horse, but his words came out with far more raw emotion than he ever intended, and rather than tease, they sounded just as serious as he meant them.

"I better get up."

Blakely had just reached them, and Journee scrambled to her feet, Dante climbing up behind.

He'd pushed her away again. She wasn't like the girls that he knew, the ones that he'd been with. Plus, he had a bit of an advantage over her, because he knew who she was.

For all she knew, he was some random football dude who had not been in her life just days ago. No wonder she was backing away.

Should he tell her?

He wanted to. But he wasn't sure whether that would make a difference. Maybe she wasn't having the same feelings for him that he was for her in their correspondence.

Or maybe that was what was making her pull away.

Regardless, Blakely offered the horse, apologizing, "I had no idea you couldn't ride. Or I would have gotten something else."

"No problem. I guess everyone around here rides. It's a natural assumption that I would."

"That's true."

"Thanks so much for bringing the horse," Journee said to Blakely, "but I think if it's okay with you, maybe Dante and I will just walk to get our tree?"

He'd managed to find the saw that he dropped on the ground, and he held it at his side. "What happened to the saying if you fall off, you need to get right back on?"

"Really? You want to get back on?"

"Sure. I think that's where I went wrong when I was a kid. I never got back on." Maybe he wouldn't be afraid of horses if he'd gotten back on when he was younger.

"Okay. If Blakely will hold the horse, I'll bend my knee, and you can use that as a step to get on."

It was a little more complicated than what she had indicated, but he'd finally struggled his way onto the horse.

"Great job!" Journee said, and it was almost like she was struggling to act normal and pretend that whatever had passed between them when they were sitting on the ground hadn't happened.

He didn't really want to do that.

But again, he couldn't blame her.

Blakely helped Journee get on, and this time, she sat behind him, her arms around his waist and her head next to his shoulder.

He kinda liked this way even better.

He did not say that to Journee though.

He managed to get the horse going—a slow walk—and they went a little ways, out of earshot of her sister, before he said, without looking around, "Sorry about that back there."

"It's okay. Part of riding horses includes falling off once in a while."

"Well, I'm sorry about that too. But that wasn't really what I was talking about."

She didn't say anything, and he got the feeling she just wanted to ignore it. But he wasn't going to.

"Sorry for going too fast. I guess...I guess I got a little more serious than you want to be. And I didn't mean to scare you."

"Maybe it's not that you do scare me so much, it's just that I was kind of thinking about someone else. And I've had a lot of fun with you today, but that other person is in the back of my mind."

"Other person?" His stomach dipped. Was there someone else?

"I've never actually met him. There's nothing between us. I just... I just feel like this isn't a good time," she finished kind of lamely.

It didn't matter to him. His heart was jumping up and down in his chest, and he wanted to smile and fist pump the air, except he didn't want to scare the horse, because a nice, slow walk was about all he could handle.

Still, his elation calmed rather quickly because they still had the same problems. Even though he knew now she was kind of interested, even if she didn't know who he really was.

But he had football, and that's what he had to be invested in, and she had her hometown and the roots that she had deliberately put down and didn't want to shift.

There was also the small problem of the fact that he couldn't really tell her who he was. Not without breaking what felt like Race's trust.

It was a dilemma he wasn't quite sure what to do about. To top it off, he wasn't going to be able to stick around and work on it. He needed to leave. He needed to get home for training camp.

Still, it was encouraging that things seemed to be headed in the right direction.

Chapter Twenty

Journee stood beside Dante as the two teens who won the Not Such an Ironman Ironman competition got ready to throw their pies.

They'd been given ponchos, but nobody was going to be aiming for their body.

"I think I'll have a hard time not ducking," Dante murmured to her.

"My reflexes aren't that good, but I think I'll close my eyes anyway. Because you're right. I'm gonna want to dodge."

The kids on the other side of the table only had to throw across maybe six feet. As they were choosing which kind of cream pie they wanted, Journee and Dante exchanged looks.

Despite all their efforts, they'd managed to come in dead last.

Thankfully, though things had gotten awkward after they'd fallen off the horse, they pretty much had been back to normal by the time they got off the horse and delivered their Christmas tree to the table.

The gingerbread house had been an unmitigated disaster. The chimney idea had been really good, but they'd been in a hurry and hadn't allowed the icing to solidify, and it had toppled. Not just toppled, but toppled off the table.

It had been impossible to piece it together from the floor, so they just basically emptied the icing container on it and made it into an igloo.

No one had ever heard of a gingerbread house being made almost completely from icing and shaped like an igloo, so, yeah. Disaster.

"I think this experience will be good for next year. Pretty sure we'll be able to whip their butts."

"You can't be serious. You're thinking about next year? You'd do this again? Voluntarily?"

"Sure. It was fun." He looked like he meant it too. He was smiling, one side of his jaw pulled up a little higher than the other, giving his grin a lopsided, almost boyish look, and she felt her chest tighten.

Never in her life before had she had the problem that she felt like she had now.

There were two men in her life; she liked them both.

It shouldn't be a problem. Dante was leaving. Leaving for football, and she probably wouldn't hear from him again until the season was over.

She didn't know much about it, but she was pretty sure he didn't have scads of free time, definitely not weekends where they could meet and do something.

Plus, there was a huge social scene involved with sports figures, a scene she knew nothing about and definitely wouldn't fit in.

She needed to think of him as a friend, and although he had kind of hinted around about more, and she'd been more tempted than she ever had in her life to just close her eyes and jump, she was glad she hadn't.

It was a decision she almost certainly would regret.

"Okay, you two," Mr. Albright said, having somehow lucked out and been not only in charge of the Not Such an Ironman Ironman Contest but also in charge of the pie throwing as well. If there was a dunking booth, he probably would have gotten that too.

Some people had all the luck.

"Look at that, everyone. Journee looks like she's excited about tasting some chocolate cream. Don't miss with the chocolate pie," he called out to the twitters of the audience.

"That's just fine by me. I don't mind standing here and watching," Dante said, and everyone laughed harder.

"Throwing me to the wolves?" she said across her shoulder.

"I'm not doing any throwing. They are." He nodded his head at the two teens who had lined up on the other side of the table from them.

Looking out across the crowd, Journee was able to see most of her siblings grinning. All of them had been where she was at one time or another, and this year was her turn.

Actually, her brother Denver had won Father of the Festival, which meant everyone in his family—and there were a lot of kids in his family—got to throw pie at their dad.

Hopefully she'd have herself cleaned off in time to be able to see that.

Natalie was supposed to be able to throw pie at her husband as well, but Journee suspected that Natalie wouldn't be able to throw pie at Denver. They'd probably end up eating it together instead or something.

Twenty minutes later, it was pretty much all over, and everyone who had participated in the Not Such an Ironman Ironman Contest had an opportunity to throw pie at them.

"It wouldn't be so bad if that lemon cream hadn't made a direct hit. I hate lemon," Dante said as they toweled off in the small equipment shed behind the diner.

"I love lemon. I would definitely have traded you that for the coconut cream. I break out in a rash from coconut."

"I don't think you're any more allergic to coconut than I am to horses."

"Nice." She looked over at him. "I think we're supposed to be supporting each other."

"I can't support falsehoods."

"Fine. You're right. I'm not allergic to coconut. But I wish I were."

"So I guess that's where I say I'm not allergic to horses..." He looked thoughtful for a moment. "Actually, I don't even wish I were. I think I'm gonna come back here next spring and get Blakely to give me lessons. I will learn to ride horses."

"I think you'll enjoy it."

"Don't you ride? I thought you said you did."

"I can. But honestly, it's never been my thing. Blakely definitely got all that in the family."

He took one more swipe with the wet towels that had been provided. "Did I get it all?" It hadn't been hard to take their ponchos off, but their heads were a completely different story. She wasn't going to feel clean until she could go home and take a shower.

"You missed some here." She reached up and with the corner of her towel cleaned his ear.

"There's some on your ear too. That must be the trouble spot."

"That and noses, I think. Although I'm pretty sure my nose is good."

"I don't see any on it." He fingered his towel a little and looked down.

She had the impression that he wanted to say something, but in all honesty, she wasn't sure she wanted to hear it. She liked the fun and the laughter, and the little bit of awkwardness when they had been thrown off the horse, but even with the slices of excitement that had cut through her, it wasn't something she really wanted to repeat.

She wanted to play it safe.

"I guess you know I have to leave tomorrow." He twisted the towel in his hands.

She forced herself to sound relaxed. "I'm glad I got to meet you. I guess I have my dad's matchmaking with Blakely to thank for that."

"Yeah, from what I hear, it's been successful. I guess they won the kissing contest."

"I heard that too."

He swallowed and shifted, and suddenly the air around them felt awkward as she thought about the kissing contest, and matchmaking, and Dante leaving.

"I know that sports figures aren't the favorite of your family, but if you could maybe pretend that I'm not a sports figure and maybe think about if it might be okay if I come back?"

She put a carefree smile on her face. "You don't need my permission to come back. Mistletoe is a great town, and I'm pretty sure everyone would love to see you again."

"Come back to you. To see you." He looked at her, and her heart twirled. She didn't want to dismiss what he had said, because obviously it was said with a great deal of feeling and also a bit of risk.

But she just didn't want to go there.

"When I told you about my boyfriend—that I only had one…" She smiled a little, thinking of Computer Geek's reaction to the fact that she only ever had one boyfriend; Dante had had a similar reaction yesterday. "The reason we broke up was because his parents were more important to him than I was. They wanted him to choose someone different."

"How long were you guys together?"

"Six years."

"And it took them six years to figure out they didn't want him to be with you?"

"I think they thought he'd come to his senses. But they finally gave him an ultimatum. I guess for a long time they'd been kind of working on him, just telling him how I wasn't good for him. I think they thought I was kind of simple, and when I decided to come back to Mistletoe and not take the job that I'd been offered in the city that paid a lot more, I guess they put their foot down and told him it was either them or me."

"Ouch."

"Yeah." She stretched her towel, carefully folding it, like it was imperative that she match the corners up exactly. "You'd think after six years, that was a pretty big time investment in a relationship, and he loved me. Maybe he did. But...when he was given a choice...he didn't choose me."

Dante looked at the floor like he didn't know what to say. Probably he was uncomfortable, because even though it'd been a while, the thought still cut. Pretty deep. Not that she was still in love with Alex. She wasn't, but the idea that she could invest so much time in him, thinking they were looking at a long-term thing, and he could decide someone else would be more important—that hurt.

"It wasn't his parents. I didn't expect him to love me more than them. But whoever he ends up with—he basically chose someone, anyone else, rather than me."

"You're not out of line to expect your man to love you more than he loves his parents. It's a different kind of love, and he can love both, but sounds to me like maybe you're better off without him, because obviously he should have chosen you over them. Maybe you dodged a bullet."

"That's exactly what I ended up having to tell myself. That it was good that I knew then that when he was given a choice, I wasn't first. It was hard at the time. But like you said, it was for the best."

Dante looked like he commiserated with her, but as she studied him, she didn't think he quite made the connection.

She pushed her hair back. It probably looked terrible. Still, she needed to make sure he understood. "I determined that I was never going to take second place in any romantic relationship again. Never."

She'd gotten the towel folded into a perfect square, and she set it down on the table, smoothing it off with her hand. "I'm sure you understand what I'm saying." Really, she wasn't sure he did.

She straightened and looked at him.

It took what felt like a long time of their eyes meeting before understanding dawned across his features.

"The football conversation," he finally said.

She nodded.

"I didn't realize that was your background."

"You explained what football meant to you. It was like your family. I wouldn't ask you to give that up. It's what has gotten you to where you are. But I guess you understand now where I'm coming from too. I did six years of second place. It was a wasted six years. I'm not going to take second place again, not in a romantic relationship."

His jaw bunched, then jutted out. He nodded, no trace of the smiles they'd shared all day and for most of the time he'd been in Mistletoe. "Appreciate you explaining that to me. I understand now. What you meant when we were talking about it."

"Yeah." Funny how she'd not known him very long, but this felt like a goodbye that was going to hurt. Maybe even one she'd regret.

But after experiencing what she had, she'd be foolish to walk into another relationship knowing that she wasn't the most important thing and knowing that he would choose something else over her.

"I guess this is goodbye?"

"Maybe—"

He held a hand up. "Stop. Don't even say maybe we can still be friends."

"Can't we?"

He looked away and rolled his towel up, then let loose with a flick of his wrist. It curled out and snapped. He looked back at her. "Does what's between us feel like friends to you?"

It was her turn to look away. Because he was right. If she had friendly feelings toward someone, she didn't have to constantly remind herself that she was only going to be friends with them.

"No," she said, soft and low, not wanting to admit that he was right but needing to give the honest answer.

He nodded. "I guess it's gratifying to know that much at least," he finally said.

She swallowed. For some reason, her throat was tight and hot.

"Then I guess this really is goodbye." His words came out with a finality that pierced through her ribs, that she didn't want to hear, but she couldn't think of anything else to say.

He snapped the towel again, with more force, frustration on his face. He started to turn away, then turned back and said in a rush, "What if I—"

"No." It was her turn to hold her hand up. "You're not giving up football."

A shadow of a smile crossed his face, and he grunted. "How did you know? And that's what I'm talking about. Right there. Do you know how rare that is? I mean, you get me. You get all of me." She wasn't quite sure what he meant by that. "I don't want to lose that. I want to fight for that."

"I'd fight for it too, but I've already been there. It's just heartache. I would hate it, because you wouldn't have time for me, and you'd be busy, and that would make me feel like I'm not really that important to you, like every single day you're choosing something else over me."

"That's only during the season. I can make time for you. People do it all the time. Half the team is married. Somehow, they make it work."

"How many of those marriages last?" she asked, not wanting to be negative but knowing she was right.

He looked away. She suspected the failure of most of those marriages was more than just not having time for spouses. She supposed there was probably a lot of temptation, a lot of dissatisfaction, a lot of women who would be willing and eager to comfort a man who was fighting with his wife.

Just guessing, since she really didn't know.

But a feeling she didn't like lay like slime in the pit of her stomach. It curled and crawled, and she hated the guilt it produced.

He's trying so hard, and you're shutting him down at every turn. Why not take this chance?

It had to be her heart speaking, because her brain was shouting no. She'd been here before, she'd cried rivers, she'd wanted to stalk Alex, chase him, beg him to take her, to choose her, to stand there again, between the two choices, and not turn away from her.

She'd become someone she didn't like.

She vowed never to do it again.

And yet...

"All right."

His head snapped up. She hated the hope flashing his eyes, which made her feel even worse.

To see him hurting hurt her.

"Let's write. Letters. We'll write to each other. We'll see if you make time for that. Wouldn't that be a start?" she asked, humbly, because she wanted to close the distance between them and put her arms around him and give him whatever he wanted, just to see his face clear and his lips smile again. She hated that the pain on his face was from her. Because of her fear, her trying to protect herself from pain.

Hated that.

She liked the hope on it much better, and the way his eyes crinkled and his lips turned up.

"Like old-fashioned snail mail with pencil and paper? That's your suggestion?" he said with a firmness that made her narrow her eyes.

"Well, yeah. It seems like a compromise. That way, if you don't have time for me, maybe it won't hurt quite so bad, and yet we're still maybe trying to make it work. Right?"

"You're right. I'll write to you. How many letters a week do you want?"

She grinned. "How many do you think?" She didn't want this to be all her.

"I'll write you when I get your letter. That day. So, you control how often."

"It's a deal."

He threw his towel on the table next to her neatly folded one. "I'm liking this, except, before, when we were saying goodbye, I was hoping for a goodbye kiss. Now, I'm trying to think of another excuse and coming up empty."

"An excuse?"

"Sure. What can I give as a reason to kiss you?"

"So that's how you do it in the city? You need a reason?"

"Oh, that's right. Out here in Mistletoe, you guys just put random strangers in a contest and have them kissing for no reason."

"That's right."

"So maybe we can start practicing for next year's contest?"

"You get points for being original." She walked closer, putting her hands on his chest.

"That feels like a yes to me."

"I think it feels right."

He smiled and leaned down, and his lips brushed her forehead before he straightened.

Her eyes had fluttered closed, but they opened, and she was sure they showed her disappointment. "That's it?"

"You don't think that would win a kissing contest?"

"Maybe in the city. Here in the country, we do things a little different."

"Oh? You want to show me?"

She grinned. "Something tells me I'm not going to be able to show you anything."

"Why not?"

"You're the one with all the dating experience?"

"So that makes me an expert? I'm not sure I can take the pressure."

"That's okay. Maybe we can figure out something new together. Something that works for both of us." She smiled, but there were definitely questions in her eyes.

His smile answered those as he leaned down. "I said earlier I was falling for you, and I kind of meant it as a joke. But it came out exactly the way I felt about it. There's something about you that pulls me, that makes me feel like I would do anything just to see you smile."

"You don't have to do anything big or special. All I want is you."

His breath wobbled, and a shudder went through him. "Simple words. But nobody ever wanted me. Outside of football."

"You know what? I think in order for it to mean something, I have to want you *with* football. Because that's such a huge part of who you are."

Tension seemed to drain from his body. "You need to come first. I get that too." He brushed his lips over her forehead again. "I'm afraid I'm not going to be perfect to begin with. Will you be patient with my mistakes?"

"I'll try," she said, as sincere about it as she had ever been. "I guess you might need to be a little bit patient with me too. I might have some baggage with the whole you need to be able to do your job to the best of your ability so you have to spend a lot of time on it kind of thing."

"Did we just admit that neither one of us will be perfect and we're going to try to make this work anyway?"

"Yes. I think so."

He brushed her cheek with the back of his fingers, then threaded them through her hair. "You have a beautiful heart."

She smiled, her heart pounding as his head bent and his lips slanted across hers. She reached up, pressing against him, sliding her arms around his shoulders and down the ridges of his back.

It was a beautiful kiss yet bittersweet, because he was leaving, and although she knew he meant every word he said, she wasn't sure that either one of them had what it took to make what they had, which was special and amazing, work.

Chapter Twenty-One

The next day Journee got up with a smile on her face.

She and Dante might have lost the Not such an Ironman Ironman Contest, and they might have gotten pies in their faces, but yesterday had been an amazing day.

It had been an even more amazing evening.

Time had never gotten away from her as it had last night as she and Dante sat on the back porch, feeling the warm summer air, listening to the crickets, and talking about anything and everything.

Later, there was kissing too.

Talking had been nice.

Kissing was even better.

She felt like she knew him. Had known him. Definitely longer than a few days.

She didn't want to let him go.

Regardless, he'd promised to write, and, he'd also promised to come over and see her this morning before he left for the airport.

So, she was ready when his car pulled up, and she definitely wasn't playing hard to get as she flew out the door and ran down the walk, making it to the side of his car before he even had the door shut.

He was quick though, and he caught her as she threw herself into his arms.

"Wow. If this is the reception I get after one night, I wonder what it's gonna be like after more?" There was a tease in his voice that made her smile, but she didn't bother to answer since he leaned down and kissed her, she kissed him back with maybe a little bit of desperation, since she knew he was leaving, and they hadn't even talked about when they'd see each other again.

Today after lunch she was headed into work. He'd be at training camp soon.

Hopefully, letters would be enough.

After a long time he pulled back, and it seemed like there was a little uncertainty in his eyes as he said, "I brought my first letter. If you don't mind, maybe we can go somewhere you can read it."

"Now? While you're still here?"

She could see him dropping off a letter, one that she could read while he was gone. It seemed a little odd he had one he wanted her to read while he was still there.

Still, there wasn't too much she wouldn't do for him. The thought was a little scary.

He nodded.

"You want to go to the back porch?" she asked, as he took her hand.

"Yes. That sounds good." He seemed to take a breath, almost as though what he was about to do was intimidating. "I don't have a lot of time before I need to leave for the airport."

"I know."

She didn't want to face the inevitable, but in some way she wanted talk about it. Really. Not that she was having doubts, necessarily, although she wasn't sure she was strong enough to keep the doubts at bay once he left.

They walked to the back porch without saying anything more

and they sat down, side-by-side, on the swing. Dante still held her hand, an envelope clasped in his other.

She thought it was going to say something, but after a few moments of silence, he handed her the envelope.

It just had her name on the front. His handwriting surprised her. Not what she was expecting, and vaguely familiar. Actually, very familiar.

It couldn't be.

Her stomach tightened and her hand trembled.

She tugged her fingers from his so she could open it.

It held a regular piece of notebook paper, and she pulled it out.

She hadn't read a word, had only allowed her eyes to skim over the paper, recognizing the handwriting before everything clicked into place, and she knew that the man sitting beside her, the man she'd spent the last few days with, the man she vowed to write to and try to make things work with, was the pen pal that she'd been matched up with, Computer Geek.

Her hands dropped her lap, and she sat, trying to catch her breath, staring at the other side of the porch, running everything through her head, trying to figure out what this meant, what *exactly*, it meant.

How long had he known? Why hadn't he told her? What else did she need to know? Had he been playing her? But why?

Even though part of her felt betrayed, the bigger part of her wanted to believe that whatever he had done, he'd done with her best interests at heart. That maybe he'd figured out who she was and hadn't known how to say without violating the promises he made when he signed up as her pen pal.

Deciding she needed to give him the benefit of the doubt, she held the letter up and read it without looking at him.

Dearest Journee (The Healing Pen),
I know you're probably feeling shock right now. I wish I

could have figured out a better way to tell you. But I just couldn't leave without letting you know.

My biggest fear is that you'll think that for some reason I was trying to trick you, or pull a fast one on you, or use you in some way. I promise, that is not the case.

I had no idea who you were — that you were *The Healing Pen* – before I came to Mistletoe.

Even after I came, I didn't know it was you until the boy and the dog ran into you and you dropped your notebook.

I wasn't prying, I promise, but my eyes just landed on the handwriting and I recognized it immediately. I didn't need to see "Computer Geek," on the top of the page in order to know that you were the person that I had been writing to.

I think I'd already been half in love with you through our letters.

Even though I didn't know how old you were, or anything about you really that would tell me whether or not we could ever be anything to each other.

I'm sure you can imagine my shock.

I'm not sure you can imagine my excitement, though.

Up until that point, I'd had The Healing Pen in my head, and yet the real live, beautiful, sweet and funny woman in front of me was burrowing her way into my heart.

I have to say it was pretty sweet to be able to reconcile the two of you into one person that I could fall in love with.

And I have. Fallen in love. With you.

I know how you feel. How you're afraid that you might not be the most important thing to me, and I have to admit, that scares me a little too.

I'm not used to depending on people, or making them so important that everything else fades in comparison.

I guess, knowing my background, you can understand how hard that is for me.

But, I hope you can also understand, I feel like you're worth it. You're worth the risk, worth changing for, worth putting first.

I appreciate the fact that you're going to be patient with me. Because I know that I'm not gonna be perfect. I love the idea that I found someone that I don't have to be perfect for.

Thank you for some really fun times, and for giving me great memories of Mistletoe, Arkansas. I plan on coming back. A lot.

Rehabbing after my car accident has been a priority for me. Being able to play football again and not letting the accident defeat me has been all-consuming.

However, I've made a decision, one I think will make you happy. If it doesn't, we could talk about it, but...I intend for this to be my last season playing football.

I found a small town where I'd like to move once the season's over, and I found a small town girl that I want to spend my life with.

I hope, she'll eventually feel the same way about me.

Love,

Dante

PS I just want to let you know, the app that you and I made together is releasing next month. Thank you.

Journee finished reading his letter and allowed her hands to drop back into her lap.

He hadn't known. He hadn't figured it out until he was here, and then he hadn't known how to say anything to her, or even if he should.

She couldn't say that she would have done things any differently if she had been the one to find out somehow that he was Computer Geek.

She absolutely could not hold anything against him.

Looking over at him, she said, "I love you too. Thank you."

The smile that she loved spread across his face. She didn't have time to say anything more, because he pulled her to him, and kissed her.

Epilogue

February 14

"I suppose we're not the first romantics to think that Valentine's Day is a really great day to get married," Journee said as she adjusted the shoulder strap of her overnight bag and walked in the cabin door that Dante held open for her.

"I think June's a popular month for weddings. A lot of my buddies told me we should wait until then. But it was hard enough to wait until after the championship game." Dante's voice rumbled behind her, a certain note in it that gave her shivers and made her stomach feel like warm honey.

Someone had lit a fire in the fireplace and there was a basket of fruit sitting on the table.

"Hard for both of us," she said, turning with a smile.

The cabin looked cozy and amazing, but she honestly didn't care. It really didn't matter where they were, or where they went, as long as they were together.

That's how she felt. She was pretty sure that Dante felt the same way.

He'd done exactly what he said — answered every single one of her letters on the day he received them — all through the football season, and even into the postseason.

She'd been happy for his sake that his team had made it to the championship game.

If she were honest, a small part of her wished they hadn't even made the playoffs, since that would mean he was home that much faster.

Home to Mistletoe. Home to her.

Regardless, the postgame celebration hadn't even started when he'd announced his retirement, and there were more than a few people who noticed he cut out and left before any celebration had really gotten started.

There had been some speculation that there was an impending marriage in his future, fueled by his teammates who had been interviewed and asked about him, or more specifically, asked about his absence.

It hadn't mattered.

"You think you're going to miss it?"

He nodded. "Undoubtably. I'm sorry, football has been a part of my life for so long. It's definitely going to leave a hole."

"I hope you don't regret the decision you made for me." She'd honestly talked to him about it – on the phone and in her letters, but he wouldn't be dissuaded.

He slipped his arms around her and pulled her close, leaning his head down and brushing his cheek against her temple.

"Never. I don't have the slightest bit of regret. And while I know that there's going to be some adjustments, for both of us, I look forward to each and every one of them."

"Maybe a coaching position will open up."

"Maybe. But it's going to have to be close because I'm living with my wife in Mistletoe."

He kissed her temple. "I have a couple ideas for a few more apps, too. I never expected our hospital app to take off the way it has. I think maybe coding can take the place of football. And maybe the high school here in Mistletoe will need a coach eventually. Think I'd enjoy coaching high school football. Or junior high football. Or peewee football. Or," he paused. "Working on creating my own football team. Yours and mine."

It took her a couple of seconds to understand what he was saying. Then she laughed.

"Eleven kids is way too much. Especially if it's eleven boys."

His lips moved a little lower, a little closer to her ear. "You don't sound very firm on that. I think the lady might be persuaded."

Her laugh was a little more throaty this time, and she pressed against him. "Maybe. I'm definitely okay if you want to try."

Join Jessie's list and be the first to know about new releases and sales on her books!

Read Heartland Joy, the first book in the Heartland Cowboy Christmas series where Shawn Barclay goes to help a friend of his dad, and finds himself defending the Bad Luck Widow against the entire town. Keep reading for a sneak peek now.

Sneak Peek of Heartland Joy

How long had it been since he'd ridden on a grocery store cart?

Shawn Barclay watched as an older teenage boy, or possibly a young man in his early twenties, started at the back end of the parking lot, pushing his cart with one foot on the back bar and one foot pushing like a skateboard, gaining momentum as he hurled across the blacktop.

Shawn held his watermelon under one arm and slowed his stride just a little, grinning.

It was a good thing he'd bought a watermelon, or he might have been tempted to join the dude in a shopping cart race.

He and his brothers had done that more than once growing up, much to his mother's disapproval.

Never in a lot that had been so busy, though.

It was unseasonably hot for October. October in Arkansas anyway.

That's where Shawn had grown up.

But for Iowa?

It was his first day here, and he wasn't sure.

Still, the watermelon would be a great lunch before he found the farm where his parents wanted him to help out over the winter.

The dude with the shopping cart must have done it a time or two before because somehow, he managed to tilt the cart up on one wheel and spin it in an entire circle before it thumped back down and he gave it two more giant pushes with his leg.

Shawn's smile had slipped, however, because a woman, her cart laden with groceries, hurried out of the store, glancing at the dark, billowing clouds rolling in from the west.

Shawn didn't think it was going to start pouring in the next five minutes, but maybe the woman wanted to get home and have her groceries unloaded before the storm started.

Regardless, she wasn't paying attention to the dude on the cart, and the dude certainly wasn't paying attention to her.

He'd developed a little bit of an audience, and he seemed to be playing to them, swerving the cart into screeching S turns before he grinned at the folks standing and watching, then shoved with two more big pushes before he rode the cart with both hands in the air.

It was at that point that the lady hurrying out of the store must have heard the commotion and jerked her head around in the direction of the dude on the cart barreling toward her.

Maybe she could have avoided a collision if there hadn't been so many groceries in her cart.

She yanked back on the handle; her frame, though slight, seemed strong and agile.

Iowa was a lot different than Arkansas. Flat for one.

The sky was huge, not hidden by any mountains and very few hills. It was farm country, just like Shawn had come from in Arkansas.

Still, it wasn't home, although there were plenty of people in Arkansas just like this woman in front of him: short, no-nonsense haircut, and despite her predicament of being directly in the way of a barreling cart, she definitely wasn't a maiden in distress, seeing the danger and working to avoid it rather than standing like a deer in headlights, waiting to be rescued.

Still, Shawn could never resist even the idea of a damsel in distress, and he ran forward, dropping his watermelon and grabbing hold of her cart, adding his weight to hers for a second or two while the dude riding toward them, finally aware there were other people in the parking lot, put all of his skills to work to try to avoid the imminent collision.

Maybe if Shawn had gotten there just a second earlier, they might have been successful.

As it was, he hit the front right corner of the cart, jerking it with enough force to spin it and throw the woman and Shawn to the right as the cart swung left.

Shawn might have been better off if he hadn't run to help at all, since he ended up landing on top of the woman, getting both feet tangled in the wheel of the cart, and tumbling to the ground.

"That didn't quite go the way I planned," Shawn muttered as the woman moved under him, grunting just a little.

He unwound his long legs from hers and stood, the jeans he wore protecting his legs from any scrapes, although the palms of his hands burned from catching himself on either side of her.

The lady, on the other hand, didn't make it out quite so well. He could see a scrape on her upper arm and some blood on her wrist. As she rolled over, both of her knees were scraped because of the knee-length skirt she wore.

He offered his hand. She grasped it, and he pulled as she leaned back against it, wedging her feet on the blacktop and stretching to her feet.

"Thank you," she said, glancing at her cart which had stopped a few feet away, before brushing herself off.

The dude who'd hit them came back with his hands in his pockets, having gotten his cart stopped. "I'm sorry about that, Bridget. I didn't see you there."

"It's okay, TJ," the lady said, looking at the brush burn on her arm which had to be burning, even though it wasn't bleeding profusely.

Shawn did a double take at the woman. "It's okay?" he asked incredulously. "The dude just ran into you. Aren't you…like, angry?"

The woman turned her head and narrowed her eyes, almost like she was angry at him for suggesting that she should be angry. "Why would I be angry? No one got hurt." She moved her eyes over him from top to bottom. "You look like you're fine…are you okay?" She asked that last question like it just occurred to her that he might have been hurt.

"I'm fine, but you're all scraped up. It's because the guy was careless. Showing off." Shawn swept his eyes around the parking lot where TJ's admirers had been gathered. They'd dispersed now, and no one was in sight.

"He was just having fun, and I'm glad he was able to." She gave Shawn another side glance before she moved her gaze to TJ. It wasn't a look of affection, exactly, but more the look of someone who'd known someone for a really long time. "How's your mother doing?"

TJ already looked abashed, and now his eyes went to the ground. "Not good. I'm here to pick up her prescription for more painkillers," he mumbled. Then he jerked his head at Shawn, who tilted his head ever so slightly in return, still jacked that the dude seemed to be getting away with being irresponsible and running into people and no one seemed to care. TJ pulled his hand out of his pocket and waved it in the lady's direction. "I'd better go get it. Sorry again," he murmured as he strode away.

The lady let out a deep breath, then turned to her cart, grasping the handle with one hand while she shook the hand with the scrape on her palm a little before touching the cart with it.

"You probably have some stones pushed up in there, and your knees are scraped up too. Do you have someone who can look at it?"

Shawn should just leave. The lady had been very clear that she was not upset, and she wasn't going to make a big deal about it.

He appreciated the lack of drama. Some people made big deals out of everything, and it got tiring. But honestly, that dude should be held accountable. He could hurt someone else if he didn't stop being so careless.

Of course, more than once, Shawn had been the one riding a cart in the parking lot, and he had been enjoying watching the guy until he had run into the lady.

If he'd run into someone though, he would have spent a lot more time apologizing and making sure she was okay. But that dude acted like he couldn't wait to get away from her.

"I'll be fine. I do appreciate your concern. But TJ's had a pretty hard summer since his mom and sister were in an accident. His sister didn't make it, and his mom is having a difficult recovery."

Shawn pursed his lips, feeling bad for TJ but not bad enough that he wanted to give him a free pass to run into anyone with a shopping cart.

Still, if the lady wasn't angry, he would try to hold his own temper. "Oh. I see. I'm sorry, I guess you have the advantage of being a hometown girl. I'm new."

"I know. I should have introduced myself. I'm Bridget Rallings." She held out her hand, then kinda shrugged and looked apologetic. "You probably don't want to shake since I'm bleeding."

Shawn took the hand she offered, but instead of shaking, he turned it over and cradled it in his. "There are a couple of stones in there." He looked up. "You never answered my question about whether or not you have someone to help you get them out."

"They'll work their way out. I'll clean them good when I get home." Her words wobbled a little, and she swayed, taking her hand out of his and grabbing a hold of the cart.

"Are you sure you're okay?" he asked. "If you hit your head, I didn't see it." His eyes scanned her body, looking for a bump he might have missed.

"I thought I was. My head doesn't hurt at all. I just had a little dizzy spell."

He glanced at the clouds. They were boiling on the western

horizon but didn't seem to be coming any closer, although there was an occasional gust of wind to dispel the heat that beat down from the sun and radiated out from the black macadam.

"Come on. I'll push your cart. Tell me where your car is. Maybe you can sit down on the bumper for a minute."

Her car wasn't far away. They passed the watermelon he'd dropped as they walked toward it.

"As soon as I get you settled, I'm going back to grab that. That was my lunch," he said, humor in his voice, as she walked slowly beside him, allowing him to push her cart but not having any more wobbles.

"I'm sure I'm fine. I don't know what came over me. I guess I just lost my balance for a minute," she said, almost seeming embarrassed that she wasn't completely strong.

She got her key out and opened the trunk as they walked toward it.

"Do me a favor and sit there on the bumper for a minute. I'll be right back." He waited for her to sit before he turned and jogged back toward his watermelon.

It was cracked, and there was a puddle of juice on the parking lot underneath it.

He picked up the watermelon, careful to hold it so he wouldn't get the sticky liquid on his hands. He had every intention of helping the lady unload her groceries into her car. But as he turned, he could see she was already back on her feet and unloading her cart herself.

He had a feeling he might not be wanted, but he couldn't just walk away, so he walked over, laying his watermelon back down on the ground beside her car. He reached into her cart, pulling out several bags.

"Is there a certain way you want these?"

"No. I didn't get any bread today, and we have our own chickens, so everything else can be put wherever," she said, humor in her voice, which was a little friendlier than she'd been before. But still reserved. "Although these bags here"—she indicated the bags in the front basket of her cart—"are for Matilda, and I'd like to keep them toward the back."

He didn't say anything more but helped her with the rest of it. As she was putting the last bag in, she either lost her balance or had another dizzy spell because her body shuddered and she fell forward. Her shoulder hit the side of the SUV.

"Are you okay?" he asked, pushing the cart away and coming to her side, putting his steadying hand on her shoulder as she straightened.

"I think it's just the heat. Maybe I turned too quickly. I feel fine."

She sighed a little, and he felt compelled to say, "How about you sit down for a minute? I'll share my lunch with you." His eyes crinkled, although he was only half joking. He didn't think there was anything seriously wrong, but sometimes a person just needed a few minutes to recover. He thought that was what was going on here, but in case not, he preferred she not get in her car and drive just yet.

His oldest sister, a surgeon, might have a different take, and if he felt like he needed a professional opinion, he wasn't afraid to text her.

He had time before the farmer he was going to see was expecting him, and while he had zero intention of getting involved with anyone here in Iowa, he wasn't opposed to making friends.

He wasn't going to be staying long enough for anything more.

A Gift from Jessie

View this code through your smart phone camera to be taken to a page where you can download a FREE ebook when you sign up to get updates from Jessie Gussman! Find out why people say, "Jessie's is the only newsletter I open and read" and "You make my day brighter. Love, love, love reading your newsletters. I don't know where you find time to write books. You are so busy living life. A true blessing." and "I know from now on that I can't be drinking my morning coffee while reading your newsletter – I laughed so hard I sprayed it out all over the table!"

Claim your free book from Jessie!

Escape to more faith-filled romance series
by Jessie Gussman!

The Complete Sweet Water, North Dakota Reading Order:

Series One: Sweet Water Ranch Western Cowboy Romance (11 book series)

Series Two: Coming Home to North Dakota (12 book series)

Series Three: Flyboys of Sweet Briar Ranch in North Dakota (13 book series)

Series Four: Sweet View Ranch Western Cowboy Romance (10 book series)

Spinoffs and More! Additional Series You'll Love:

Jessie's First Series: Sweet Haven Farm (4 book series)

Small-Town Romance: The Baxter Boys (5 book series)

Bad-Boy Sweet Romance: Richmond Rebels Sweet Romance (3 book series)

Sweet Water Spinoff: Cowboy Crossing (9 book series)

Small Town Romantic Comedy: Good Grief, Idaho (5 book series)

True Stories from Jessie's Farm: Stories from Jessie Gussman's Newsletter (3 book series)

Reader-Favorite! Sweet Beach Romance: Blueberry Beach (8 book series)

Blueberry Beach Spinoff: Strawberry Sands (10 book series)

From Strawberry Sands to: Raspberry Ridge (12 book series)

Swoonfully Jolly Holiday Stories:

Holiday Romance: Cowboy Mountain Christmas (6 book series)

Cowboy Mountain Christmas Spinoff: A Heartland Cowboy Christmas (9 book series)

New and Much Loved: Mistletoe Meadows (4 books and counting!)

Laughing Through the Snow: Christmas Tree, PA Sweet Romcoms (6 short reads)